I0520435

THE SORRY LIFE OF
BOBBY CHASE-THE-LORD

By Oscar William Case

This is a work of fiction. All characters, names, events, etc., are the product of the author's imagination, except that where there are real names, they are used fictitiously unless it is a historical fact. Any other resemblance to characters, names, events, etc., living or dead is purely coincidental. This book or excerpts therefrom may not be reproduced in any form without the author's permission except short excerpts may be used in reviews.

ISBN-13: 978-0-692-90083-3
ISBN-10: 0-692-00083-7

Oscar Case Books

Other books by the author:

The Stranger from the Valley
The Upamona Gold Claim Wrangle
Blood and Blazes in Upamona
The Bloody Gulch
Posse Justice
The Man from Hanksville
O'Shaughnessy's New Deputy
Trouble at Sagrado Ranch
Western Stories – A Collection of Short
Stories

THE SORRY LIFE OF BOBBY CHASE-THE-LORD

CHAPTER ONE

Bobby Leaves Home

"Clyde, I'm leaving here one of these first days to start my own church. I've learned from your Pa about everything there is to know about conducting church meetings and I'm fed up living in Dry Creek and cleaning your Pa's barn. I'm disgusted, too, now that I'm older and understand what people think about Indians, me, in particular. They hate me and I don't care for the likes of them either."

Young Clyde Sweeney and I were cleaning the Sweeney's barn on the outskirts of Dry Creek for another church service. This town was a mining and ranching town in northwest Utah Territory that I had grown to hate.

I leaned on the push broom, my eyes on Sweeney. At eighteen or twenty years old, I want to get out of Dry Creek to bigger places and things. I swiped money from the donation pot, even a five-dollar bill, to live on until I find a job or get some from preaching.

"Where do you think you're going to go?" Clyde moved a chair to the row in front of the podium. He didn't look my way.

"I'll hitch the stage to Great Salt Lake City where all the people are. There ain't nothing around here except farming and ranching, and I don't own neither one. I ain't going to work for nobody but myself after I leave."

"Them miners made Salt Lake City sound mighty interesting before they cleared out," said Clyde, moving another chair to start a new row. "Pa would never let me go, and I ain't goin' to run away."

Feeling like I had just struck gold, "I'll come back to see you in my new suit that I'm going to get in the city."

"Nobody's goin' to attend a church run by a brown-skinned Cayuse Indian who is poor as a turtle dove." Clyde smiled and his eyes scanned me.

"I won't start preaching right away. I'll look around for an assistant's job first, before I kick him out and take over."

"Ha, ha, ha, you been bit by the Glory Bug."

"You'll see."

The next Wells Fargo stagecoach leaving Dry Creek found me, Bobby Chase-the-Lord, sitting on top of it, hanging on for dear life as the four horses pounded down the road leaving the town fading in the dust. No one was inside the coach.

"No Indian is goin' to ride inside," said "Whip" Willets, the driver. "That space is for white people."

I clambered up behind my friend riding shotgun, Kid Ferry, who rides free for protecting the stage against holdups and Indians. He got me a good price, telling the station manager I was his helper. Hell, he never rode shotgun in his life and I'll bet he never does it again.

I didn't say anything, but I was madder than Hell. I had just as much right to ride in the coach as anyone else, since I paid half my passage. Willets headed the horses south, down the trail through the small valley. The white salt to the south shone and glistened. A person had to turn his eyes away to avoid short-term blindness. I had trouble with it, but I couldn't get over the extent of the salt flats. I kept staring, amazed at the distance it covered. It blended into the landscape until I couldn't distinguish salt from sky.

"How far is Great Salt Lake City?" I asked.

Willets and Ferry ignored my question.

I made myself as comfortable as the roof would allow and leaned back on my gunny sack of clothes and personal effects I stole from the Sweeney house. I avoided looking directly at the sun and concentrated on the mountains in the distance.

One of the miners told me, "That range of mountains over there is the Grouse Creeks," which could be seen from Dry Creek. To the south and east, I could barely make out more mountains with small humps protruding into the sky. Out to the west another row, mostly lost in the waves of heat, were beginning to be visible and confusing my sight of them. *Were the humps there or not?*

"How far did you say it was to Great Salt Lake City, Mister Willets?" I asked again.

Kid answered after turning around and taking in the spectacle of me bouncing up and down trying to hold on. "It'd be about two hundred miles, so just git comfortable and quit asking dumb questions. We'll be looking for the California Trail, where we turn left and go northeast toward the Sawtooth Mountains. We go east from there."

Hah! Kid Ferry is supposed to be my friend. He must be trying to impress Mister Willets, telling me all this stuff. He's doing it for nothing.

Around dinnertime, when the sun was high in the sky, Willets stopped for the second time to rest the horses in a clearing by a small clapboard building and corral. A lone cedar tree grew among the sage brush surrounding the open space. A well and water trough sat out front where the stage parked and the horses were watered. An old, gray-bearded man came out to greet the stagecoach driver and unfasten the traces. Willets and Kid climbed down and gave the old man a hand. The old graybeard herded the horses to the corral behind the cabin.

"I was wonderin' how we were goin' to get through it without dyin' of thirst," said Willets, looking at Kid and turning his gaze to me. I was still on the roof of the stagecoach. "You, Indian, you want some water? You gotta get down and get it. Make it snappy, we ain't goin' to wait all day."

"My name is Bobby Chase-the-Lord. You can call me Bobby," I said, climbing off the coach and smiling at Willets. "I worked for Reverend Sweeney in Dry Creek, and I'm going to Great Salt Lake City to become a preacher for the Lord."

Willets and Kid laughed out loud and looked at me like I had just told a funny joke.

Irritated and edgy, I aimed my old revolver at Willets, saying, "This is for you, Willets, for not letting me ride inside," and shot him in the head.

He fell to the ground, dead. I turned to look at Kid, "That'll teach him to be nice to Indians."

I aimed the revolver at Kid.

"Grab his gun, Kid, and drag him into the cabin. Go through his pockets and take his money, and get us some food while you're in there. We'll take the old graybeard with us when he brings the fresh horses."

Graybeard returned with the harnessed teams and backed them into place on each side of the wagon tongue, hitched them up, and said, "What was that noise I heard? Was somebody shootin'?"

"I shot at a crow and missed" I said.

"What? My hearing's bad. Speak up, Laddie."

"Get in the stagecoach! You're going for a ride!" I yelled as loud as I could, pointing my revolver at his chest.

Graybeard jumped in fright when he saw the gun. "Don't shoot and quit p'inting that thing at me. I'm gettin' in the coach right now. I need a rest anyway."

Returning with a gunny sack in his right hand, Kid said, "Nobody's goin' to be travelin' this road for a while. Nobody goes to Dry Creek anymore, since the mining companies shut down and moved out." He tossed the bag through the open window at the old man, who held up his hands to stop it from hitting him in the face.

I stuck the .44 down my waist behind the belt buckle and opened the stage door. Stepping on the coach frame and holding on with my right hand, I reached for my sack on the roof. Wrapping my fingers around the top of the bag, I dropped to the ground. Opening the bag, I reached in and found my belt and holster, let the bag fall, and buckled the belt around my waist. I shoved the instrument of death into its resting place and said to Kid, "Let's go."

Kid climbed into the driver's box. I grabbed my bag of possibles and climbed up beside him, resting my feet on the bar that ran across the front.

Staring at my eyes, Kid said, "I've taught you well, Bobby. The law will be on our trail when they find Willets' dead body in that house. When we git to Salt Lake, I'll teach you more tricks to go along with your quick trigger, but don't order me around like I was yer servant. We are good friends, and let's keep it that way."

Kid turned his head and yelled at the horses, and slapped the reins on their backs. "Hiya, hiya. Git a-movin'."

The coach slowly pulled away from the house and Kid pulled the reins to the right to get back on the trail.

"What kind of tricks you going to teach me, Kid?"

"Things like pickin' pockets and cheatin' at cards and things that'll be useful."

"Reverend Sweeney would have one of his conniption fits if he knew I just killed a man. But, like I told you the other night, I'm sick and tired of all his hootin', hollerin', and ordering me around and making me sleep in the barn like one of his animals, and all the damn Whites calling me Injun and treating me like a dog. An eye for an eye says the Bible.

"That life is behind me, thanks to you, for teaching me how to shoot and ride a horse and all that stuff about being a bad hombre, stealing and rustling cattle, and cheating all the time. Those days and nights I sneaked off and met you in Peg Leg's bar is going to be worth it. I'm a grown man now and I can do what I want and to Hell with everybody."

Squinting his eyes against the glare of the sun and licking his lips, Kid said, "Wow, you done took after Sweeney with all that fancy talk. I think you'll make a fine preacher. I'm just as happy to be away from them mines that I was roped into. I'm no miner. I'm just a ramblin', rustlin', thievin', cheat-at-cards, lyin', no-good cowhand that owed a debt, and now I'm free of it and ready to get on with a new life. Ya-hoo!"

"Hey, up there!" yelled the old man with his head out the window, "Where's Whip? What did you do, kill him?"

"We're just borrowing his mud wagon!" I said in a voice loud enough for old graybeard to hear. In a normal voice, I added, "We'll drop you off somewhere along the trail. Is that what we're going to do, Kid?"

"Sounds good to me. Take a look in Willet's bag, here on the floor. Maybe he has something to eat in there so we don't have to stop."

CHAPTER TWO

Arrival in Great Salt Lake

A week flew by and Kid Ferry and I were relaxing in a room at the Western Hotel on Third West Street in Great Salt Lake. The room had only one bed, a settee, a chair and a night stand with a pail of water and a pan on the bare wooden top. Our saddles and gear were piled in a corner. It looked like a fine room to me, since it's the first hotel room I ever saw.

"I told you selling those horses was a good deal," said Kid, lying on his back on top of the bed with his head on the pillow. "It got us some money to partake of fine things like the luxury of sleepin' on a soft bed instead of a pile of hay in someone's stinky barn."

"But now we don't even own a horse between us," I said, still not relaxed and standing at the one window gazing out at the waning light of dusk. "After we set fire to the stagecoach, we had to use the horses to get into town. I didn't mind that at all, but now we have to walk any place we decide to go. I wonder if that old man made it to the next station. He was pretty old and rickety when we dumped him out in the middle of the night between stage stops. He stumbled and fell. Of course, it was dark as the insides of a black bear."

"He'll be all right. A tough old horse thief like him. Why else would he be working out there alone? To get away from people that's why," said Kid. "I know a horse thief when I see one."

"Maybe."

"You're too much of a pessimist, Bobby. Didn't I tell you I was goin' to teach you some things? Things that will git us some money right away, and we can locate some good targets for robbery, too. We about spent all the money buying suits, shirts and boots. And old saddles and ropes and harness for horses. We'll get us some good horses too."

I turned away from the window and sat down on the comfortable stuffed chair.

"With all these people around all the time, how we going to rob anybody? That would just bring more lawmen on our tails," I said, with my dark eyes on Kid. "Do you think they know about the stage and Mister Willets yet?"

Not waiting for an answer, I moved back to the window and stared down at the street below watching the pedestrians.

"They won't know who they're lookin' for, since we got all cleaned up and some new clothes and a haircut. I signed us into this hotel under another name, but I ain't goin' to use that one anymore. My name ain't even Kid Ferry. I was just usin' that while I worked off my debt in the mines. What kind of a name do you want Bobby? One of those bohunk names of the miners or Eye-talian? What sounds good to you?"

"I'm dark-skinned, so it'll have to be something that fits. I don't want no Mexican name. The Whites hate Mexicans as much as the Indians." I stared out the window with the evening growing darker.

I can't get over the gas street lights, having never seen one before. Crimany, all the people walking up and down on the sidewalk in the dim light of evening. Where they going? Out to dinner in a fancy restaurant or to one of those fancy theaters we saw or home? I never seen so many people in my life, not even back in Oregon, and I ain't ever been in a town this big before. If the Sweeney's could see me now, they would have a conniption fit. I feel awful guilty for killing that man, Reverend, but he deserved it. Even you wouldn't have put up with him calling me names and treating me like a beggar.

I will pray to the Lord for forgiveness, but I ain't going to take it anymore. Kid and I are starting a new life. I'm sorry I never told you about Mister Ferry, Reverend. We deserve to be treated better. I thank you for teaching me the language and the church and about the Bible. I'll put all that to good use the first chance I get.

Reluctantly and with a deep sigh, I turned away from the window and prepared for a good night's rest on the settee.

Kid shook me awake in the morning with the sun up and his shadow falling across my legs. I noticed how tall the Kid looked from prone position, taller than me by a hand's length. His red hair, uncombed and curly, stood out in the light coming into the room. It looked like it was on fire, all bright and glistening.

"Wha…What? Oh, it's you, Kid. I guess it's time to pull on my boots and hunt up something to eat huh?" I mumbled, trying to wake up.

"You bet it is. Today, I'm goin' to learn you how to pick pockets and eat good food without payin' a dime for it. Rise and shine, me bucko!" said Kid, smiling and showing his even teeth below a thin, red mustache. "We're goin' down the street to that café we saw yesterday coming from the stables. I need some ham and eggs or something."

"I'm all for that," but, I wondered about picking pockets with my big hands. My Indian name is Imekes Ipsus, 'Big Hand'. I've never told it to anyone. I don't want the White people to make fun of me. Bobby Chase the-Lord is bad enough.

I crawled out of bed and dressed in the new black suit.

"We'll leave our guns here. We won't be needin' them," said Kid. "And after we eat, we're goin' to find you a nice blue or black gown like churchmen wear and a white collar to wrap around your neck, so you can start preaching the Word. And I'll show you how a pickpocket works. We can always use extra money."

"You got the day all lined out. I'm anxious to start spreading the Word of the Lord. Let's go."

Being dressed in my new outfit made me feel like I had nothing to worry about as far as the law was concerned. The new suit and boots and string tie made me look like a flourishing rancher or at least a clean, honest cowboy in town on business.

We left the hotel and headed for that café.

"Here it is, Kid. We almost went past it," grabbing Kid's arm and pointing him toward the entrance. I smiled, my mouth barely open and my lips stretching and putting a crease in my brown cheeks that I could feel. Right now, I'm one happy Indian.

We never got around to changing our names.

CHAPTER THREE

Eats a Free Breakfast

Kid pulled the café door open, saying, "Let me do the talkin'. We might get a free meal out of it."

The place was crowded with early, hungry customers. We made our way to the rear and found a table by the kitchen. No sooner did we get seated than an older woman with grayish-black hair emerged from the kitchen and smiling, asked, "What are you having, boys, coffee, water, postum, or tea?"

"We'll have a cup of postum, Ma'am, that darn Mormon stuff," said Kid, admiring the woman and making a quick judgment. "We don't have any money to pay for it, though. We got robbed on the train. Somebody went through our bags while we were sleepin' and stole our money, Ma'am. We're on our way to the LDS warehouse to work. We're awful hungry, aren't we, Bobby?" He smiled and winked at the still-attractive waitress.

"The boss'll get mad at me givin' his food away, but you look like nice, clean Mormon boys all dressed up in your suits and such," said the waitress. "I'll be right back."

"Look dejected and hungry Bobby, and don't laugh," warned Kid, looking around at the customers.

I looked up and saw a partially bald man with brown hair combed over the top of his head, sweating, looking at us through the window in the kitchen door with his bright blue eyes.

I quickly looked away and swallowed the moisture in my mouth, sighing.

The waitress reappeared with a tray on which sat two glasses of water and two cups of hot postum with steam rising in the sunlight coming through the front window. Holding the tray by the edge on her left arm, she served our postum and water and let the tray drop to her side.

"My boss is in a good mood this morning, fellas. You can order anything you'd like up to a dollar-and-half." She smiled pleasantly and smoothed her white apron with the free hand.

"Gee, thanks, Miss. What's your name? I like you already," said Kid, winking his right eye.

"I'm Alberta. Bertie is what everybody calls me, boys. What'll you have to eat?"

"Well, by golly, Bobby, hear that?" Kid laughed. "I'll have a stack of flapjacks with a half-pound of bacon, Bertie, with lots of butter and syrup."

"I'm hungry enough to eat a raw pig, but just bring me the same," I said, smacking my lips and smiling.

We devoured the pancakes and bacon, thanked Bertie and left.

"That only works once in a eatin' place, Bobby, unless yer alone. Them older waitresses like to be complemented and fawned over, but they have to be careful or lose their job. We won't eat here for a coupla days, and we'll pay next time and leave a nice tip fer Bertie. You never know when you'll be needin' somethin' to eat."

"I get your meaning, Kid. What we going to do now?"

"We're goin' to that Mormon factory warehouse and work for 'em long enough to find a nice robe we can steal. I think by lunchtime we'll find what we need. We'll git a free lunch and tell 'em we can only work fer another hour, 'cause we gotta go to the Temple grounds to see a bigwig fer our Bishop down home."

"You think we can get away with stealing right under their noses? Won't they see us and call the law on us."

"Stick wi' me buddy, and you'll see how easy it is," said Kid grinning at me. "We'll use a different name to check in there, real common ones like Bob and Ronnie Jones, like we're brothers. Yer my half-brother, how's that sound?"

"I guess it'll do." I wasn't convinced walking side by side with my compadre. "How did you know about that warehouse and where is it?"

"Let's see if this feller knows. You just keep walking," said Kid, accosting a well-dressed man coming toward us in the typical black suit. "Excuse me sir, could you tell me where the LDS factory warehouse is?"

The man, a couple inches taller than Kid, gave him a dirty look as he eyed him and said, "Yer almost there, young man. Go down Third West to Fifth South and turn west fer a block. You can't miss it."

"Thanks, Mister, and good day to you," I heard Kid say.

Catching up with me, Kid slipped something into my hand saying, "Hold on to this in case that man starts after us."

I gave the object a quick glance, seeing a wallet, and said, "How did you do that?"

"Easy, it was real easy, and before we leave town, you'll be able to do it, too. Let's hurry and git around the corner."

We tried to be unnoticeable as we walked fast down the street, passing the slower pedestrians and nodding to another now and then. Kid, running by the time we reached Fifth South, turned the corner. I tried to keep up as Kid dodged into the first building doorway. It was a shoe shop.

Breathing hard, I closed the door behind me, turned around and peeked out through the big glass window to make sure no one followed us. The shop smelled of old musty leather, glue, and sweat. Light from a lantern hung over the counter and melted into the light from the front window. Kid was sitting on a bench in front of the small counter. I plopped down beside him, saying, "Whew, I ain't used to moving that fast." I took a deep breath and stared at Kid.

Kid paid no attention and waved his arm at a man behind the counter taking a customer's money and dropping it into a large cash register. The customer left and Kid piped up, "Howdy, my man. Can you measure me for a pair of fancy cowboy boots? I need a new pair." He grinned and watched the man step from behind the counter and approach the bench.

"You musta been in a big hurry to get here," said the man, laughing and reaching into his right rear pocket for a measuring tape. He had a large belly under which he wore a black belt to hold up his black pants. He wore a newly ironed white shirt and elastic arm garters.

"We were just taking a fast walk to git the blood flowing, Mister, like we do every morning," said Kid, breathing heavy. "I'm taking my left boot off so you can measure that foot. It's a little longer than the right one."

"Not unusual, sir, not at all." The big, paunchy man bent over to measure his foot. "What color leather do you want? Brown, black, or a mix of each n a fancy design for a foot eleven inches long and four wide?"

"Ya got any red leather you could add to a black cowboy boot?" Kid asked, watching the man stand straight, raise his shoulders, and exhale a long breath.

"I could dye some leather for that purpose, say, a trim along the top and a toe of red. How does that sound? Of course, I'll have to charge extry for the dyeing, but I guarantee it for the life of the boot."

"How much money ya talkin' about? I'll put some away for it."

"I could make the boots for about sixty dollars is all. When would you like to pick 'em up?" looking at Kid and glancing at me.

"I'll be back in town in about three weeks and can ya sell me a bottle of the black dye?" said Kid, getting up from the bench and moving to the counter.

I walked the few steps to the front door and watched the people going by.

"Here's a bottle of dye for a dollar, and I'll make out a slip for the boots, Mister...Mister...uh...," said the bootmaker.

"Rex, Gandolphus Rex, is the name. Most people call me Dolph."

"Rex, huh? Fine, Mister Rex, here's your receipt for the boots the next time you're in town."

I turned to watch Kid take the receipt and stick the bottle of dye in his jacket pocket.

Kid said, "Don't sell those boots to anyone else. I'll pick 'em up around three weeks from now. Thanks a bunch." He turned toward me and added "Let's go, bud."

CHAPTER FOUR

Looks for a Preacher's Gown

We continued walking in the direction of the LDS warehouse without saying anything until we came to Fifth West. We stopped to let the wagons pass by and started across the road when traffic slowed.

"What did ya buy the dye for, Mister Rex?" I asked and laughed, waiting for a horse and wagon coming down the street at a fast trot.

"I'm goin' to dye my hair when we get back to the hotel and shave off my pretty mustache in case I should bump into that guy again, the one I stole the wallet from," said Kid, feeling in his pocket for the dye bottle.

"You sure know all the tricks. When you going to pick up your new boots?" I grinned.

"Maybe in six or eight months, if ever," Kid guffawed, his cheeks turned reddish. "That's the only thing I could think of to explain why we were in there."

"Ha, ha, ha. You could've told him you wanted to know where a fine saloon could be found or a nice restaurant. I wouldn't mind a bit eating in one of those places."

Still chuckling, we made it across the street and headed for the next stop. Arriving, Kid told me, "Let me do the talkin' again," while reaching for the door.

"I wouldn't miss it for anything, no sir. After you, Mister Rex."

Inside, Kid headed to a window in the back wall of the hallway and rang a bell that was resting on the window shelf.

"Hello, hello! Anybody in there?" Kid yelled, and we waited and waited. Kid rang the bell three more times.

A man came through a door in the back wall of the office and approached the window with a curious expression on his wrinkled face. "What can . . . "

Kid interrupted, saying, "Good morning, good morning. My half-brother and I were sent here to work a day for our ward. I'm Elder Bobby Jones and this is my half-brother, Bill, also an Elder in the church. We would like to..."

"Hold on, Mister Jones, just a dag-blasted minute," said the man, looking us over through the window. "Now...what ward are you going to be working for?"

"We're from down south, a place called Idle Springs. The Bishop is J. F. Smith and it's a brand-spanking-new ward. We were sent up here by him to deliver a message to Mister Brigham Young about the ward, but Mister Young died a couple days ago, so we gave it to a man in the office. We were told to report in here and do work for the Lord. We would like to work in the clothing department, if that's all right. The Bishop said the ward needs clothes for the poor and indigent and we'll earn credit for our work. That's what he told us, right Bill?"

"That's right." My eyes opened wide, listening to Kid. I coughed a couple of times to keep from laughing. I wondered how Kid knew so much about the Mormons.

"Well, Elder Jones, we don't normally let the people pick and choose, but it just so happens today we need some help in the clothing department," said the little, stooped man. "Let me write your names down and the ward you're from, and I'll get someone to show you where you'll be working."

A few minutes later found us hanging clothes on hangers and putting them on a rack under the sharp eye of an elderly matron who was short and heavy in her black dress and shoes. She never stopped grinning while she explained what we would be doing.

"I think you boys got the hang of it," she said. "If you have any questions, I'll be over there along that wall doing the same thing."

When she disappeared in the racks, Kid stopped in the middle of putting a brown, wool coat on a hanger and dropped it back into the cart. He gave me a knowing look and a shake of his head and began going through the racks of clothes looking for a garment that he thought would fit an up-and-coming preacher-to-be.

I continued hanging skirts, dresses, coats, and other items, keeping one eye on Kid fumbling among the racks.

It took some time for Kid to come alongside me looking like he had just won a poker hand. "I found just the thing to do your preachin' in, Bobby. Look at this."

"A blue dress! I ain't going to stand on a street corner in a woman's blue dress." I stared at Kid, agitated. "Can't you find anything better than that?"

"Don't worry. We'll take it to a dressmaker and have it cut to look like a robe and fixed to match your small body. No one will know the difference."

"I don't know whether to trust you or not. If it don't look right, I ain't going to wear it."

"It'll be fine after it's made to fit, believe me." Kid looked around to make sure no one was listening. "I'm goin' to slip it under my coat. It's time for lunch."

We got in the line of workers going into the lunchroom. As Kid neared the door, he suddenly veered out of line, saying, "You go on and eat and put a sandwich in your pocket for me. I see trouble in there. I'll meet you outside at the corner on Fifth South." He left before I had a chance to say a word.

Later, I spotted him leaning against a building and smoking a cigarette, a practice that I had never tried, because Reverend Sweeney had railed against it more than once in his sermons. A sin of the Devil, he said.

"What happened?"

"The man I took the wallet from was in there," said Kid. "This place is getting too confined for me. I think we should get out of the big city and settle down in a small place that don't know us. I got a hunch that our faces will be plastered all over the big towns before very long. Every lawman in northern Utah Territory will be gunnin' for us as soon as someone finds the remains of that stagecoach."

"I don't know. I haven't done any preaching yet, and I don't plan on killing anymore, either. I have to set an example, if I'm going to be talking other people into joining my church."

Kid stared at me and waved his right arm in the air. He relaxed, his eyes still on me. "Yer church? You don't even have a church yet or a building fer people to come to. How you goin' to get the money for a church building? I say, stick with me and I'll help you, and maybe I'll even be a member of your church. What're you goin' to call it?"

"The Church of His Holiness Under the Trees. See, I won't need any building right off. I'll start preaching on the streets and in the parks, if there are any, until I get fifty or sixty members signed up. With their donations, I'll find a building. Come on, let's go to the hotel."

"That's not much of a plan. It may take you a year or two to get that many reg'lar donatin' members," said Kid, flipping his cigarette on the sidewalk and stepping on it.

We set out for the hotel by crossing Fourth West, dodging horses and wagons. Neither of us said anything until I opened the door to our room. I let Kid enter first.

"Holy cow!," exclaimed Kid. "What have we here?"

Staring at a man lying on his back on top of the covers, I asked, "Who's that on the bed?"

"Hey, wake up, you drunken no-good!" yelled Kid, grabbing the man's shirt and pulling on him.

There was no response and there would never be from the corpse. He was dressed in a pair of brown wool pants, a green and black checkered shirt and dirty brown work shoes. He had a gray mustache and beard, and shirt-collar length, grayish-black hair. A black felt cowboy hat with greasy spots on the brim rested on the floor.

"Who do you suppose it is?" I asked. "He could be a drunk, a miner, a farmer, a ranch hand or who knows from the way he's dressed."

"I don't have any idea. How did he get in here? The door was locked, wasn't it?"

"I just stuck the key in the lock and turned. Maybe it was already open and he just wandered into the wrong room and died," I speculated.

"Let's turn him over and see if there's any blood leakin' out," said Kid, pulling an arm with one hand and the other under a hip. He had him turned over before I could help.

"Wow! Would you look at all the blood and he's still got a knife stuck in him," I said, starting to turn peckish. "I gotta sit down before I pass out."

"We better put him back like we found him and git the Hell out of here," said Kid, pulling the body back to its original position. "Pack yer bag quick-like. They'll probably say we did it and hang us, even though we're innocent. Let's go!"

"Our guns are still here. They must've been in a hurry, and our money, too. Thank the Lord!"

We left the hotel sneaking past the desk without paying, loaded down with our saddles and bags.

CHAPTER FIVE

A Visit to a Post Office

It began to rain as we left the hotel. We rented three horses at the stable, saddled up, and headed south with our belongings packed on the third horse. We didn't have anything to say for the first few miles in the drizzle. Kid was silent for a change. Although he didn't kill the drunk in the hotel, we knew the law would be after us since we vacated the room with no explanation to anyone. Where do we go now to make ourselves scarce? As far away as we can get in a week, preferably in the mountains.

I concentrated on the future. I want to get started on my preaching before we end up hardened criminals and always running from the law. That ain't the life I want. I should never have killed that stagecoach driver. If they find out I was the one who did it, I'll never be able to become the Man of God I want to be and that Reverend Sweeney said I should be.

We rented our horses with no intention of ever bringing them back. We'll sell 'em to someone down the line and steal some good ones. The law will add that to the wanted posters. I'm a horse thief as well as a killer. Maybe Kid will tell me how he came to be an outlaw or why he does things that are considered breaking the law. Thinking about it for a moment, I asked him, "Where are you from, Kid?"

"I don't know why you want to know, but I skipped out of an orphanage in Saint Louis, Missouri, and made it to Kansas City when I was nine years old, and I been on my own ever since. I became an expert at begging for things I needed to survive – meals, money, a job, a place to stay and other things. Kansas City was my training ground and there were plenty of older beggars, scalawags and thieves to teach me things after the Civil War ended.

"I turned sixteen and thought I better make tracks out of town before the law caught up with me. I headed to Colorado and found a job on a large cattle ranch west of Denver. In time, I became a fine horseman and learned the methods and manners of handling a large herd of cattle. But I couldn't give up my bad ways of stealing and cheating at gambling, which got me in trouble again. I was caught slipping cards from the bottom of the deck in a poker game by a fellow card player and had to shoot him or be killed. I took off for the high peaks of the Rocky Mountains west of Denver and became a miner.

"The mining boss asked if I knew how to use a pick and shovel, because what we have here is a gold mine, or it will be when we hit the vein of gold." He was a big, ugly cob with a thick, black mustache, wearing a miner's cap with a gas light on the front.

"He told me, we need workers bad, so you can go to the tool shed and arm yourself with a pick and shovel and a miner's hat, and go into the mine shaft and report to Cap'n Slade. Go on git out of here.

"And my life as a miner began, Bobby. I became good friends with a man named Pacheco. That's all I ever knew of his name was Pacheco. Pacheco this, Pacheco that, just plain Pacheco. We worked here for six or eight months, looking to get our share of the gold, but we hadn't hit the vein when Pacheco said it was a waste of time. I was good at card cheating but he was expert at it, and I owed him about a thousand dollars when he said we were leaving. I promised to pay him and to keep him from killing me, I told him I would work it off in the next mine.

"We're going to Utah Territory, he said. There's a mine just started in a place called Dry Creek near the Great Salt Lake and it's just full of silver and copper and things like that. You'll only have to work a few months to pay me back with all the silver we can steal. It's better than bein' dead, ain't it?" he asked.

"I reluctantly agreed because he had been a good friend. We drew our last pay and headed across the Rockies to Dry Creek. I could have killed him any time, but I liked him and enjoyed cheating at cards with him. I paid him back and he gave me two hundred dollars just for being honest. I have a new partner to teach all the things I learned from Pacheco and others. This is going to be fun, Bobby."

I stared at him sideways in the light rain. He was smiling and looking ahead.

"We'll go somewhere where we can make a new start," I said, telling myself maybe Texas or California, and we won't steal from anybody. "Let's head to Texas and get away from this place, far away, before the law catches up with us. By the way, that wallet only had twenty-two dollars in it and that won't get us far. What did you do with it after I gave it back?"

"I still have it in a saddlebag. I'll dispose of it along the way somewhere, maybe, or I may keep it. It's a nice money carrier. As for Texas, we'll think about it. For now, we have to get lost and find us a dry place to hole up for a while. Let's hear some of yer preachin', so I can see if yer goin' to be good enough to make us some money to put with that twenty dollars."

"I've practiced a little speech in my mind. Here goes.

"My friends and fellow citizens who believe in the righteousness of the Lord, gather around and let me introduce you to the Church of His Holiness Under the Trees. We are a new church who believes that Jesus the Lord created His church outdoors where He did most of His preaching. Just look in the Bible and Jesus is mostly out in the bright sunlight, and the sunlight is what He wished to bring to the common people of the World. That is what we want to do, bring sunlight to the people through His teachings. We would be ever grateful for a small donation to our cause. Even we must gather in a few seeds in order to grow the church and bring it to all the deserving people."

Bobby Chase-the-Lord eyed Kid riding along comfortable in the saddle.

"What do you think of that opening, Kid? I thought it came off just fine."

"That was a good start, but you have to practice, practice, practice until you get it memorized frontward and backward, and you must show that you know the Bible the same way," said Kid, looking toward the cut in the mountains, closer now, but still a few miles away.

We continued south down the middle of the valley, approaching the small farming settlement called Murray. We could see a smelter smokestack in the distance with its gray plume of smoke issuing from the top.

We came to the town center and noticed a post office sitting by itself on the road through town. It sat on a small hill above a stream flowing in from the east.

"Let's stop here and check out this place," said Kid, pulling his old gray horse to a stop. "South Cottonwood Post Office. One of us should go in there and read the Wanted bills on the wall to see if our pretty faces are posted yet."

We both dismounted and tied our horses' reins to the hitch rail.

"I guess I'll go look around in there. I ain't never been in a post office. I'd kinda like to see what it is," I said, staring at the door and pulling my trousers out of my boots before stepping onto the boardwalk.

"I got a hankerin' to take a look, too," said Kid.

Inside, looking through the delivery window, Kid said, "You got any packages for a Bobby Jones, Mister Postmaster?"

"Don't have anything by that name," said the man. "Where's it coming from?"

"Denver. My sister told me she was goin' to send me a new pair of boots. I told her to send them here, since we would be passing through."

"Lessen you got a mailbox, I'm afraid I can't help you We haven't had any mail from Denver the last month. It's always pretty slow from there."

I stared at the Wanted posters on the wall.

"It's kind of quiet around here, ain't it? We didn't see hardly anybody on this side of town as we were ridin' in," said Kid. "Anything interestin' on that wall, Bud?"

"I don't see anybody I know that's wanted for anything."

The postman said, "It's pretty quiet here on Thursdays after lunch. Everyone is working or taking a snooze."

Kid pulled his revolver and rested the butt on the counter aiming at the postmaster.

"Why don't you open that door to the office before I plug ya? My friend wants to take a look around in there, don't you, Bud?"

I was startled at his actions, and seeing Kid was serious, said, "Yep, I sure do." I grabbed the doorknob and gave it a shake and a twist.

"I haven't robbed anyone today, Mister. Git your shanks to that door and let my friend in. We're in a hurry to be on our way. Hurry up."

I watched Kid lean way over the counter through the window and hit the man on the side of the head, knocking him backward a couple of steps and making him blink a time or two.

The postmaster hurried to the door and turned the key.

I pushed the door open and stepped into the office.

"What am I looking for? Packages, money or something else?"

"Nothing, just hold yer gun on this feller while I grab a rope."

I didn't like the looks of what was coming next, but I held my old Remington aimed at the postmaster and waited for Kid to return.

"Keep him covered while I tie him up," said Kid, returning with a rope. He closed the front door and came into the office.

"Just a minute! What you fellers think you're doin'?" said the postmaster, standing calmly, and watching us. "There ain't any money in here. It's a slow day."

"We'll be the judge of that," Kid said. "Turn around and put your hands behind your back."

Kid bound the hands together and pushed the man into the only chair. He wound the rope around the man's chest, pulled it tight and made a knot. He tied the two feet together and ran the rope around the legs of the chair and tied it securely to a back leg. Kid pulled a handkerchief out of his back pocket and stuffed it into the open mouth of the postmaster. He dragged the chair into the corner away from the window, where it couldn't be seen unless the person stuck his head in.

I stood quietly watching Kid and seeing my future as a preacher become more of a dream than the day before. I moved the barrel of my revolver to point at the Kid, saying, "Why're you doing this? I thought we were finished with unlawful crimes when we left the big city."

"We can't let an easy cherry pickin' slip through our hands, not while we're on the run. When we get clear of this valley, we'll be through breakin' the law. Put your gun away and look through those boxes in the wall for money or anything else that's worth something. C'm on. Hurry up before someone comes in."

Without saying anything, I started going through the mailboxes. I was getting a little excited doing something unlawful. My heart began beating rapidly. I quickly searched the three envelopes I found with no luck finding any money, just letters from to friends or relatives of the writers.

"This is a waste of time. Let the man loose and let's get out of here," I said.

"Sh-sh, someone is coming in. Stand in front of this guy with your pistol on him and I'll see who it is," said Kid, his face taking on a serious expression.

"Good afternoon, Madam. Beautiful day, isn't it?"

I listened and imagined Kid putting on his best face and smiling to speak to the lady.

A nice female voice said, "I was just going to say hello to Mister Sarky. Where is he, and who are you?"

"Just helping out for a few minutes. My uncle is takin' a break. Do you need some stamps or something?" Kid asked.

"No, no. I'm going to check my mailbox for a letter I'm expecting. Thanks, anyway."

I wished it was me talking to her, she sounds real pretty.

After a pause, she asked, "Mister Sarky is all right, isn't he?"

"He's fine just fine, and he should be comin' back any minute," replied Kid. "You can check your box and not worry, Miss."

In a few seconds, she was gone.

"Let's get out of here. It's been a waste of time except for the ten or twelve dollars I found in the cash drawer," said Kid. "We'll leave him tied to the chair."

CHAPTER SIX

A Girl is Attacked

Back on the road, I said, "How do you expect me to become a preacher, if you keep doing things like tying up that old postal clerk? They'll hang us both, if we don't start living within the law like everyone else."

"I know, Bobby, but I couldn't pass up a sittin' pigeon like that. I'll tell the law you didn't want to do it, but I forced you, and you can still go about being a good Christian."

"If that don't beat all. We rob the Post Office and assault that old man and you're going to tell the sheriff that I'm innocent, when I was right there holding my paw over that old feller's mouth so he won't let out a squeak. I think you would've shot that pretty girl and thought nothing of it, if she'd seen what was going on."

Kid turned to face me. "Yep, I might've. You worry too much, Bobby. The Lord sent me here to protect and watch over you, so we can do as much mischief as we like."

I changed my position and looked at the high Wasatch Mountains to the east, thinking I could reach out and touch them. The sun was playing on the rocks and cliffs, outlining every defile, turning the trees black and the cliffs a dim red. I turned my head to the west, staring at the Oquirrhs sloping up from the valley floor to the tops of their peaks, not reaching as high as the Wasatch. There in the distance flowed the Jordan River. The Mormons named it that. It carried little water, not very wide, snaking its way down the valley. Kid looked at me and shook his head from side-to-side.

"We're goin' somewhere where nobody knows who we are, and you can preach to yer heart's content," said Kid, smiling.

"Those who never practice end up a failure in life, so says Reverend Sweeney," I said, putting on what I thought would be a sad face to anyone looking at me. I loosened the reins and urged my horse to speed up. I pulled ahead, leading the spare horse.

Silently riding for a spell, I stopped my horse and waited for Kid to come alongside. Looking ahead at the placid scene by Utah Lake of the tall green trees and bushes with sun dappling the leaves and putting some of the trees in shadows, a movement caught my eye. I stared, unbelieving, as Kid's horse trotted even with my useless bag of bones.

"Look ahead in that stand of trees, Kid. It's a woman struggling with two men. Come on, let's help her."

I hit my old nag with the reins and raced ahead. Looking back, I saw Kid give his horse a slap over the flanks. The animal took off with a jump that surprised Kid. He held on and passed me. My horse wasn't so energetic, but he began chasing Kid's horse. Kid was yelling at the men holding the woman when I caught up. My heart was beating fast and my nag was breathing hard and sweating like he had run a fast mile.

"What's going on here? Release the lady afore I blow your heads off!" yelled Kid.

I saw each man grab an arm of the woman, holding her tight. They stared at Kid, each with a hand on a Colt in a holster.

"T'ain't none o' yer business, stranger," said the tall, skinny one with long black hair and a beard. "She's our sister and we're taking her home. Ain't that right, Junior?"

"That's right. She done run off again and we finally caught up with her. We're taking her home," said the shorter man who also had black hair and a beard.

I watched the woman struggle, trying to pull her arms free from the grips that held her. She moved her head from side-to-side, and tossed her long brown hair against the taller man's face. She sure is pretty and has the bluest eyes I ever seen.

"Turn her loose or your name is Mud," I said, dropping off my horse and facing the trio.

"What're you goin' to do about it, Injun?" said the tall one, pulling his revolver.

He didn't quite have the gun free of the holster when I shot a bullet into his right shoulder. He let go of his gun and grabbed his shoulder with his left hand, releasing the girl's arm.

"Yow!" the man yelled in pain. "Ya got me, you cheatin' snake!"

The shorter man held onto the girl's other arm and didn't try to pull his gun. Kid had him dead in his sights.

"Now, let the girl loose," said Kid, "or I'll let you have it between your crooked, ugly, black eyes. Get their guns, Bobby, and we'll hear what the lady has to say."

I did as I was told and said, "Get away from the girl. Move over into the setting sun, where I can keep my eyes on you."

"You stinkin' redskin kil . . .," the short man started to say. I plugged him in the throat. Blood spurted over his beard and down the front of his clothes. He dropped to the ground, moaning and dying.

"Don't call me those dirty names, you feeble-minded son-of-bitch," I swore at the dying man on the ground. "I'm sorry, Jesus, for losing my temper, but no one's going to call me names again. I pray that I will be forgiven."

"That's it, Bobby! Now yer preachin'," yelled Kid, still on his horse and holding his gun on the tall man.

The girl let out a yell and fell to her knees in the dirt under a tree. She began sobbing and moaning with tears running down her face while holding her hands over her eyes. Her shiny, brown hair was touching the ground in front, falling over her shoulders and spilling over her back.

"O-o-h, you killed him," she wailed. "Thank God, they were about to take advantage of me. You came along just in time."

Kid dismounted, keeping the tall one in his sights, and walked to the young woman.

"Stop that wailin' and carryin' on, lady. Yer safe now. We'll haul this other owlhoot to the first sheriff's office we see and tell 'im what he was doin' to you," said Kid in a quiet and solemn tone. "Who are those crooks anyway? We could tell they aren't yer brothers."

Still crying and blathering and holding her hands over her eyes, the girl said, "They're the Castanat brothers, the biggest troublemakers around Idle Springs that you ever did see. They just happened to run into me as I was going home."

She paused to suck in her breath and drop her hands. She continued, "Say, I know who you are. I saw you in the post office at South Cottonwood earlier today. You said you were helping your uncle. Ain't that right?" She brightened up, put a smile on her gorgeous lips and stood up.

"That's right, Miss. We were helping out my uncle," said Kid, smiling back and giving me a knowing glance. "What's yer name? We'd like to know before we escort such a pretty lady home to Idle Springs."

I thought that was a real coincidence, Idle Springs, huh? I smiled.

"My name is Daphne Merik."

"Well, Daphne, we better git goin' before it gits dark. You can call me Kid Ferry and my partner is Bobby Chase-the-Lord, a Cayuse Indian from Oregon. He don't take kindly to being' called names."

I tied the wounded Castanat brother's hands behind his back and helped him on his horse. A rope was tied to the saddle horn and around Castanat's waist to make sure he didn't get off the horse.

Kid and the girl loaded Junior on his horse sideways, his legs dangling on one side and his head on the other. Blood was dripping from the hole in his throat.

CHAPTER SEVEN

They Meet the Sheriff of Idle Springs

Kid, staring the sheriff of Idle Springs in the eye, said, "We've been travelin' two nights and a part of a morning to deliver this immoral outlaw to you, Sheriff. He and his brother was tryin' their best to do more than put their dirty hands on Miss Merik on the trail to Great Salt Lake. Lock 'im up and throw away the key."

"Me and Junior was just holding her up on her feet, Sheriff," said Castanat, looking at the man with the star on his chest. "She fell to the ground when she got off her horse and my brother and I took her arms and made sure she didn't hurt herself. That was all we were doin', when these two hombres rode up and shot Junior afore he had a chance to say anything. Junior bled to death."

"What did Junior do that you had to shoot 'im, Stranger?" asked the Sheriff, scratching his head and blowing his nose. He stood on the wooden sidewalk in front of his small office inspecting us astride our horses.

Kid stared at him and said, "That crook is lying," Sheriff. "I didn't shoot nobody. This feller's brother tried to kill us fer interruptin' their dirty pleasures and Bobby here, beat him to the draw. It was unfortunate that the bullet hit 'im in the throat area and he died."

"That's right, Sheriff Tubbins," said pretty Miss Merik, blinking her eyelashes and looking at a gap in the sheriff's shirt over his large belly. A missing button exposed his long johns. "Junior and Serge were fixin' to take advantage of me and these gentlemen came to my rescue. If Junior hadn't pulled his gun, he wouldn't have been hurt. The Castanats have always tried to get me alone and they almost succeeded."

"Let us pray to the Lord that we found her before she was assaulted," I said, dismounting and untying the rope around Serge's waist and the saddle horn.

Kid dismounted and took the reins of Junior's horse and tied them to the hitching post. He pulled Junior's body from the saddle and let it drop to the ground. He kept his eyes on it, making sure Junior wasn't going to get up and run away.

We were all watching Kid's progress and didn't notice Serge turning his horse with his legs and letting the animal race down the middle of the short street. He disappeared around a corner of a building before anyone could get his thoughts in order.

"Wat the . . .," said the Kid, turning his head to see the man and horse disappear.

"By damn, he's excaped!" said Tubbins, watching the rider turn the corner down the road. "How did he do that?"

Staring at Junior's body lying in the dirt among the horse droppings and small rocks, I said, "The Lord acts in mysterious ways, especially when you least expect it."

I moved my eyes to the only one with any sense, Daphne Merik. Still on her horse, she took off after Serge.

The sheriff ran down the middle of the street, yelling, "Let 'im go! We'll catch 'im later!"

Kid and I climbed on our horses and followed the girl.

****

As a Sheriff, I was perplexed. These strangers turned up at my door with that older Castanat feller wounded and that pretty Miss Merik, Dale Merik's daughter, and Junior Castanat dead on the back of a horse. Helluva way to start a day. Nothin' ever happened like this in Idle Springs before. And that Injun claiming to be a preacher of the Gospels. By God, I never heard of such a thing. Do I lock him up or let him go free? What about Castanat? Was he tellin' the truth? That means that stranger is lyin', and I'll have to throw him in jail.

I returned to the small crowd, huffing and puffing, and stared at the corpse lying in the road. Raising my head to look at the bystanders, I said, "Nordell, go see if Doc Sycamore is in his office and tell him to come and git Junior out of the road before he gits stomped on by a crazy horse."

Hearing a commotion, I turned my eyes in the opposite direction of the sudden departure of Serge Castanat. A lone rider came racing toward the group of bystanders. Before I could wipe the sweat off my face and nose, Castanat slowed to a lope, yelling, "Don't bury Junior until you hear from my Pa, Sheriff!" and kicked his horse with his feet, disappearing around the same building again.

At that moment, Daphne's horse slid to a stop. She climbed from the saddle, saying, "My horse came up limp Sheriff, darn it, and Castanat is getting away. Here come those two men that saved me. They'll never catch Castanat with the old nags they're riding."

I watched that red head and the Injun plow to a stop near Daphne. The red head dismounted and said, "Which way did he go this time, Sheriff? Our horses are worn out and we'll never catch up with him without changin' 'em. We'll go look for him as soon as we can."

"I don't know how he's able to stay on with his hands tied behind him," said the Injun, gazing at the small crowd that had gathered near Junior's body. "May the Lord carry his soul to Perdition!" He climbed off his horse and stood facing me.

"We'll catch that scoundrel later," I told them. "Let's go into my office I got more questions to ask you, Daphne, and your two friends. Doc will take care of the body."

I turned and stomped across the sidewalk without looking back. I went directly to my chair behind the desk and dropped into it with a long sigh. Daphne and the red head followed and stood watching me remove my hat, exposing my partially bald head with a fringe of black hair hanging down to my shoulders. I hung the hat on a nail in the wall behind me. I sighed.

The Injun came in and closed the door softly behind him.

"Now Daphne, er, Miss Merik, you told me that the Castanat brothers, neighbors of your family, were trying to assault you before these two men showed up. Is that correct?"

"Yes, it is."

"Do you know these two men?"

"I didn't," blinking and trying to smile, "and I still don't know exactly who they are, but they came along just in time, Sheriff. If they hadn't shown up. I would have been attacked for sure."

Looking at the red head with a steady gaze, I said, "Just who are you? I've never seen you around Idle Springs before."

"My name is Ferry, Sheriff. I don't have a first name, so everybody calls me Kid Ferry. Me and Bobby, here, Bobby Chase-the-Lord, were just travelin' south looking for a nice little town to settle down in and find a job. Bobby is a preacher and he preaches the Word of God like no other human bein'. He's from Oregon and claims he is a Cayuse Indian. He was picked up by a White family when he was very young and adopted by them. He speaks good English."

"You two aren't on the run from the law, are you?" I asked, my steady gaze still on the red-headed cowboy. He sure don't look like a crook, but who knows? The Indian, you just can't trust 'em.

"Why, heck no, we're upright, law-abidin' citizens, Sheriff," smiling and looking in the sheriff's eye. "You can ask Miss Merik about that, huh, Miss Merik? She saw us helping out a postmaster up in the Murray area."

"That's right, Sheriff Tubbins," said Daphne, fluttering her eyelids. "They were working in the post office. That's where we lived before moving to Idle Springs. My Pa sends me up there at least once a month to see if we have any mail left over. He's been expecting a package from back east for a long time."

"I see," switching my gaze to the dark-skinned one. "An Injun preacher huh?"

I looked him over from his flat black, cowboy hat to his new boots, and back up to his face. I paused at the waist to take a look at the old, single-action Remington in its holster and noticed his hands. Migod, I ain't never seen any as large as that. What the . . .? "A preacher carrying a gun don't make sense to me. I thought men of the cloth were supposed to preach against killin', and you shot Junior Castanat dead."

A knock on the door gave me a sudden start. The red head started to pull his revolver, but stopped when I have him a quick glance.

"Come on in," I yelled.

I watched the door as it opened slowly and in stepped Dale Merik, an average-sized, clean-shaved man, wearing farmer's overalls, a blue chambray shirt and an old, black felt hat. He took off the hat and said, "Doc Sycamore told me that my daughter was in here, Sheriff. She ain't in trouble, is she?"

"She ain't in trouble, Dale. What else did Doc tell you?"

Daphne went to her father and hugged him.

"He was loading Junior Castanat's body into his wagon and didn't say anything else," said Dale, tightening his right arm around Daphne's shoulders and keeping his eyes on me. "She didn't shoot 'im?"

"She might have, if she had the chance. She can tell you all about it. You can take her home."

"Come on, Pa let's go home. I'll cook us up something to eat. I'm hungry all of a sudden." She turned toward the still open door.

"If that Castanat kid done anything to you, I'd shoot him myself, if he wasn't already dead," said Merik, staring at the other men before he led her out.

I sat quietly until the door closed behind the Meriks.

"I'll have to get a posse together to go after Serge Castanat."

"We'll go after that outlaw Sheriff, as soon as we can git a change of horses," said the red-headed one. "You know someone who has some horses for sale?"

"You might try Curly Daniels. He usually has a horse or two that he don't need. You can find 'im about three miles southeast of town." I stood up and pointed at the wall behind my desk where a large map of the area was pinned. "Daniels' ranch is right here on the map of the County." I moved my finger to the spot on the map.

'And I expect that Castanat will be headed into the area around Fish Lake. His Pa and brothers own a ranch in the foothills not too far from there. No reason why you can't go along. Why'nt you come back here in, say, two hours and we'll go huntin'. In any event, don't leave town for a few days, I have some more questions to ask."

CHAPTER EIGHT

Kid Ferry is Made Sheriff

After buying some new horseflesh, Kid and I rode into Idle Springs as Serge Castanat and three other men were leaving.

"There he goes again," said Kid. "Let's chase 'em."

"We'd better stop and see what happened. It looks like the sheriff got shot. He's lying on the sidewalk," I said.

Pulling up in the middle of the road, dust flying and lifting as high as the horses' haunches, we dismounted. Leading our four-legged transportation to the hitch rail, we tied them up with a slip-knot. "That Castanat is a brazen feller, ain't he?" Kid opined.

"Nobody would have ever thought he would come back here and shoot the sheriff after this morning," said Ned Pritchett, the Honorary Mayor of Idle Springs. "His last words were, 'Ned, appoint that Kid Ferry to take my place. He seems like the type that can. . .' That's all he said."

We glanced at the crowd of spectators in front of Tubbins' office looking at the Sheriff's dead body lying with one leg bent awkwardly under him and the other boot heel resting in a pile of fresh horse manure in the road. His upper body stretched out on the boards of the walk with his big belly sticking up in the air, his bloody head resting on his hat.

Doc Sycamore drove up in his one-horse outfit and asked Ned and another man to help him lift the corpse into the buggy. I was closest to it and I grasped the Sheriff's right arm and shoved my other hand under the shoulder and pulled Tubbins to a sitting position. The other man and I lifted the body. He had him by the legs, and I grabbed him by the shoulders. Poor old Tubbins was soon in the buggy, lying behind the only seat.

"Why those dirty, stinking skunks, they killed him," I said, staring at the body. "May the Lord take his soul into Heaven's holy resting place."

The Mayor, appearing mighty pensive, watched us observing the corpse. He stared at Kid and said, "Some of us want you to take over for Sheriff Tubbins, but, I'd rather appoint anybody but you as Sheriff. However, I'll think on it."

I looked at the crowd around the buggy. Everyone was in a state of shock with the killing of their beloved sheriff. I saw four riders whipping at their animals and racing toward us down the road. Doc was climbing into the buggy and the mayor was saying something to him. The riders passed, slowing down and shooting wildly into the crowd.

Kid and I hit the dirt beneath the buggy and hoped no one got hurt. Kid wasted no time in pulling his own shooting iron and letting loose at the four men riding away. Two of them fell off their horses, dead before they hit the ground, and another yelled, "I'm hit, Serge!"

Serge kept traveling and was soon out of range and heading through the sage brush, riding low in the saddle.

My revolver was out, and I let loose a string of shots aimed at Serge disappearing in the distance. The man who was hit turned off in another direction, and no more shots were fired at him. I crawled from under the buggy and saw Mayor Pritchett stick his head up and look around at the crowd. One man had a hand to his shoulder, and another sitting on the sidewalk, held a hand to his leg.

****

"Doc, take a look at Herod and Samuel. I think they're the only ones that got hit," said Ned. "We're sure lucky that nobody else was hurt."

Herod Watkins, still holding his shoulder, said to the mayor, "Didn't you see them strangers shoot those men off their horses and wound another one? That was some shootin', Ned. And two more bodies for the Doc."

"I thought somebody shot back, but I couldn't see who it was. I was hiding behind the buggy and didn't see anything," said Ned.

"That's where I'd expect to find you. With Tubbins out of the way, I think them boys would make good lawmen," said Herod, watching the doctor pull open his shirt to look at the bloody hole in his shoulder. "They got my vote."

"We came back to join the posse," said Kid. "We ain't had any excitement for a while."

Ned was watching Doc examine Herod and didn't say anything.

Kid spoke up again, "I said, is the posse ready to git on the trail?"

"Uh, pardon me, gents, I was watching the Doc work," said Ned, turning his attention toward us. "Sheriff Tubbins said I should make the one called Kid the new sheriff. I been thinkin' long and hard about it and I've decided that I will appoint him as sheriff of Idle Springs for a probationary period of thirty days. If he pans out well enough, I'll make it a permanent appointment. Any objections from you men on the sidewalk?"

Trace Schneider spoke up, "I was kinda hopin' that I'd be the sheriff when Tubbins quit, Ned. You know that I always volunteered to help him when he was in trouble, and I showed up here today to be in his posse."

Ned was silent for a moment. He stared at Trace and the other men and moved his eyes to the two strangers in town and said, "Mister Kid Ferry, I appoint you sheriff of Idle Springs for a one-month trial. Here's the sheriff's badge, and you can appoint your own deputy for which I recommend Trace Schneider. Will you take the badge, Mister Ferry?"

Kid looked at Bobby and thought over the offer. "Well, I don't know too much about the law, but I might know the difference between right and wrong, so I'll give it a try, Mister Mayor," said Kid, with a big smile on his face. He glanced at Bobby and winked. "And I'll accept Mister Schneider as my deputy, providin' I can also have my partner, Bobby Chase-the-Lord, as another deputy. Does that sound reasonable, Mister Mayor?"

"It's a deal! Now, catch the Castanat gang and bring them in dead or alive," said Pritchett in a loud voice, making sure everybody heard. "Good Luck!"

CHAPTER NINE

Hunting the Castanat Gang

We ain't too familiar with this country, Trace," I said, sitting on a boulder and staring ahead at the pine-covered mountains and their cliff-strewn peaks. "We lost Castanat's trail back a few miles so where do we go from here?"

"Some lawman you are, Indian. Sounds like you're lost," said Schneider, standing on the edge of the drop-off watching Kid and me. "Sheriff Tubbins told me once that the Castanat brothers had a hideout in these mountains. It could be anywhere from Twelve-Mile Flat on the north to Mount Mervine on the south or even down in the Thousand Lake Mountain area. He said to go into a narrow canyon with a stream running from it and follow that stream about a mile to a small clearing. Their cabin is at the high end in the thick trees. That's all he told me."

"Hell, we might find a hundred canyons with a stream flowing out of 'em," I said, "and it'd take us a year or two to go into all them. We followed that gang for the last two days going in all directions until we lost 'em in the rocks. They led us on a wild-goose chase. We should return to town and wait 'til Serge shows up. He don't know there's a new sheriff and he'll just come into town with some of his men to buy supplies and such. What do you think, Kid?"

Returning from a walk in the woods, Kid opened his mouth to answer the question. Two bullets whizzed over his head and zinged into the tree branches. He fell to the ground and yelled, "Somebody's shootin' at us!"

More lead filled the air near the Kid and Trace. Kid stood up and ran for the trees followed by Trace. I laid on the ground where they left me, unhurt. I pulled my revolver from the holster and struggled to my feet, looking to see who was warming his pistol.

"There he is, down that hill below us!" I yelled, aiming my instrument of death down the hill and firing three rounds at a man hiding in the boulders. I had never seen him before today. He wore a tan-colored western hat and I glimpsed a black beard, before he got out of sight behind a big boulder.

Kid and Schneider came alongside, and I stepped back from the edge of the cliff to be out of the line of fire from below.

"He's in that pile of boulders behind be largest one with his horse."

"I'm goin; to sneak up on him from where the hill drops back, so he won't be able to see me," said Kid. "Keep him occupied by pluggin' away at the boulder while I get down there."

Trace peeked down and fired a couple of .44 rounds in that direction.

I shot at the man's hat as the skunk tucked his head down and got out of sight. I shot at the boulder a couple more times before reloading, making sure I didn't kill the horse. Trace shot at the boulder again and moved to a new position. The next time I took a peek, the skunk was on his horse and racing toward the bend in the dry creek at the bottom of the hill.

Kid got off a shot that missed before the rider disappeared from his sight. The skunk was out of range anyway, a waste of ammunition.

The shooting over, Trace and I mounted our horses and rode to the bottom of the hill leading Kid's horse. Everything was quiet. Kid was standing by the big boulder where the skunk had been hiding, looking at the ground for anything that he might have left behind.

"That coward got away as clean as a whistle," I said, watching Kid. "Are we going after him?"

"Trace is the only one of us who knows the lay of this country beside those outlaws, and he don't know exactly where their hideout is, so for now we'll just let 'em git away and not take a chance of getting' ambushed," Kid said, still looking at the point where the skunk disappeared. "Serge and his gang of brothers and outlaws have us outnumbered for the time bein'. We'll return to Idle Springs and wait for 'em there."

I said, "Maybe we can find some place to hang our hats since we don't have a place to sleep. If that sneaky coyote comes into town, we can nab him and throw him in the hoosegow. During the meantime, I can set up my church and do some preaching. It's always time for the Voice of the Lord. And the Lord added to the church daily those who were being saved. Acts 2:47. These outlaws must be saved, so they can be added to the church."

"Ugh," or something like it came from Trace. "Don't tell me this gun-totin', new deputy is a Bible-thumpin' preacher. It's too much for my weak mind to handle. Let's git on back to Idle Springs and hope Castanat comes to town for supplies."

Still on his horse, he said, "You boys comin'?" and headed up the hill.

"We're right behind ya," said Kid, turning his horse up the incline.

On top of the hill Trace pulled his horse to a stop and sat waiting in the trail for us to join him.

"Ya might have a parley with Dale Merik. I hear-tell he has a cabin he uses as a bunkhouse for the men he has workin' fer 'im, but there ain't nobody in it right now," said Trace, watching us come alongside. "He might let ya take it over for a little help on his two-by-four outfit."

"How far out of town is it?" I asked. "We can't be too far away in case there's some excitement that needs a lawman."

"Probably a mile-and-a-half out to the south," replied Trace, smiling. "There's just him and his daughter tryin' to make a livin' out of the dirt down there."

"Say, Trace, is their anybody livin' around here named Smith?" asked Kid. "J. F. Smith?"

"Not that I ever heerd of. Why?"

'Oh, nothin'," Kid said, smiling or was it a smirk. "Just wondered."

I didn't say anything, but I laughed, remembering he had told somebody that J. F. Smith founded the town.

Concentrating on the trail and our own thoughts, it was a silent ride into a setting sun when we neared Idle Springs. Trace slowed his horse and said to Kid, "Before we get into town, you take the road going south to the Merik's farm and it's about a mile or mile-and-a-half down that way," pointing. "Jist stay on the road and you can't miss it. I'm taking the road north to home."

"Thanks, Trace," said Kid, looking at him. "We'll be in town bright and early tomorrow. You can drop in any time before noon and we'll make plans for the next few days."

Having reached the road he was talking about, Trace gave us a wave and headed north.

"Well, Bobby, maybe we'll git to see that pretty Miss Merik soon. I hope her dad is goin' to be accommodatin'."

Our horses at a walk, we reached the Merik place just as the sun was dropping behind the mountain to the west. The short trip on the road, or to put it more exactly, the rough trail through the sagebrush denoted by wagon tracks, soon changed to willow trees and cottonwoods by a small stream with a gurgle of water.

The trail started climbing little by little over a series of small hills with the creek making its way around each hill. Our path took us into the foothills on a large flat piece of ground covered with grass watered by that same trickle entering from higher up. Birches, cottonwoods and willows grew on the banks, along with bushes and other normal growth you would expect to find where there is enough water to support them. In the light of dusk, the sight was not pretty as it got darker.

The Merik house, which we could barely make out from the trail, was another quarter mile in a clearing surrounded by cedars and pinon trees on the flats. Approaching a gate, Kid and I were jolted out of our silence by shots from a rifle that whizzed by our heads.

"Hold up there and don't come any closer!" a female voice carried through the dusky night. "Who are you and what do you want?"

"This is Kid Ferry and Bobby Chase-the-Lord. We came to see about a cabin that we heard was empty. We need a place to stay for a while. We're coming on in!"

"Don't try any tricks or I'll let you have it with this rifle! Come ahead slow and stay on your horses!"

"If you shoot, you'll kill the new sheriff of Idle Springs or his deputy," Kid said, approaching the front of the house. "Trace Schneider said you may have a cabin we could rent, and we're desperately in need of a place to take off our boots and grab some shut-eye."

"It's you, all right, Mister Ferry," said Daphne, rising from her position behind the bushes planted along the front next to the hitch rail. "I'm sure glad it wasn't that useless gang of thieves of Serge Castanat. Two of 'em came by here and threatened to burn us out if we didn't pack up and get out of Idle Springs. Pa told 'em we weren't going anywhere, and they knocked him down, jumped on him, and hit him some more. I don't know why anyone would want this place."

"Why don't you put down that piece of artillery and we'll dismount and take a cup of coffee with you or if you haven't had supper, we'd sure like to join you. How's Mister Merik doin'?"

"Pa is in bed licking his bumps and bruises them cowards put on him, but he'll be up and around in a day or two," she said, and opened the front door. "Come on in and I'll warm up some beans and throw in some bread and a cantaloupe fresh off the vine. That's about all we have to eat right now."

"Sounds like a biblical feast to me the way my stomach has been growling," I said, rubbing my midsection. I took off my hat and followed her into the cabin with Kid trailing behind.

"Can I talk to your father a minute Miss Merik?" Kid asked. "Maybe he can help identify those skunks that beat him up."

"He's probably sleepin'. His room is down that hallway there, the first door on your left. If he's awake, he'll talk to you."

The house was an oblong five-room affair with the front room taking up the area from wall to wall. The hall was on the right side of the house past two rooms and to the kitchen. I followed her and Kid, and wandered to the kitchen. It appeared to be the same size as the front room and held a wood-burning stove in one corner on which sat a coffee pot. A large dining table and eight chairs made up the bulk of the furniture. Against a wall sat a cupboard and a smaller table for food preparation or other use.

Daphne followed me to the kitchen, where she told me to take a seat at the table. She disappeared through the back door and returned carrying a cantaloupe and some raw potatoes. I hadn't eaten anything for a few hours and my belly button felt like it was rubbing my backbone.

****

"They was the Castanat twins, Willie and Wylie, that beat me up," uttered Mister Merik from his bed. His face was white where it wasn't bruised or cut. "They both had beards covering their faces, them cowards. I just finished milkin' my cows when they rode up sayin' they wanted to parley. They began cussin' at me, telling me I better hightail it out of Idle Springs. Wylie yelled that his father wanted this no-good ranch for his cattle.

"I told 'em I wasn't movin' fer anyone. They climbed off their horses and Willie knocked me to the ground. They both jumped on top of me and I couldn't do nothin' with Wylie holdin' my arms pinned to the ground and Willie hittin' me with his fists. I nearly passed out when Daphne shot at them and missed. They jumped up and shot back, but nobody hit anything, thank God. They hopped on their horses and rode away. Daphne said she thought she winged one of 'em, but couldn't tell for sure. She helped me up and led me to my bed and here I lay. That's about all there is to tell you, Sheriff."

"Why, them dirty polecats, pickin' on an ole man," said Kid, looking at the beat-up face of Merik. "First thing tomorrow, me and Bobby are goin' to make a call on the Castanats. How many are they anyway? I thought we were up against only that Serge after Bobby shot his brother. We heard he went back into town with a gang. Who are they, Mister Merik?"

"Probably Willie and Wylie and their cousins the Barnetts. There's a passel of them, too."

"Where is their ranch from here? It can't be far if they want to take over your place."

"It's over that ridge to the northwest, along the trail you came up here on," said Merik, his good eye half-closed and the other one swelled up so he couldn't open it.

"Thanks. I'll leave you alone so you can git some rest," Kid patted Merik's left shoulder and left.

CHAPTER TEN

Sheriff's Office A-Shambles

The sun hadn't come up when we brand new lawmen crawled out of our bunks and proceeded to dress in the dim light of a small candle that Kid lighted. I finished pulling on my boots, stood up, and walked to the front door and opened it. I stared into the dark, hoping the Meriks were up, but no light shone through a window. I stood in the doorway, my eyes trying to penetrate the blackness. Bushes rustled and I stepped out and moved to the side. I couldn't identify the noise until I heard a grunt and realized there were more than one or two deer nearby.

Looking at the sky, it was beginning to show a tiny bit of light to the east. Returning to the cabin, I watched Kid button his shirt near the table on which rested the candle. A glob of wax in a small dish held it upright. He blew it out and joined me standing in the dim light coming through the open door.

"There's some venison over that way in the cedar trees and brush within range of a rifle," I said, pointing in the darkness. "I'd shoot one but what would I do with all that meat? I should've asked Daphne – I mean Miss Merik – if they needed meat."

"You should've shot one. We don't have anything to eat."

"We don't have time Kid. If you're ready to travel, we'll saddle up and go into town. We might find some eggs and ham there. I think I saw a sign that said 'Food' on one of the buildings. Come on."

The horses were in the corral behind the barn. I walked the short distance downhill to the small stream and waded across. Kid jumped over it.

"My boots need to shrink some to fit," I said.

"You should've stuck your head in the water, maybe that'd clear it some. Are you ready to go into town and see what's goin' on? You seem half asleep."

"Let's stop in and see if Miss Merik is all right and ask her about her Pa."

"There ain't any light on in their cabin yet. Saddle up and let's ride."

Half-serious, I said, "Maybe I should stay here in case those rowdies return. Old Merik is still stove up and she is practically all alone."

"She's got that rifle and two pistols in the house. She can protect herself. She almost shot us last night."

"Right, then, let's go."

I could see the valley as the sun crept across the landscape. I couldn't tell how far away the western mountains were with the light playing tricks. They appeared close enough to reach out and touch, before you realized they seemed to be backing away as you rode toward them. The small hills covered with green mixed in with the gray of the sagebrush and an occasional flash of light glancing off a stream was a beautiful sight to behold. A coyote was tagging along out in the sagebrush. Maybe I'd drop a piece of jerky and see if he notices, if I had any. He looks like he could use a good-sized beef steak.

Riding through the open gate in Merik's fence, we turned north. I could see the rooftops of Idle Springs poking above and between the trees. The birds were singing, a small band of wild pigs could be heard grunting in the sagebrush, and the occasional jack rabbit popped up and ran away.

"It's a beautiful morning. I hope that gang don't ruin it."

Kid said, "I'm ready to deal out some justice if they come into town and cause trouble."

It sounded like he felt the power of being a sheriff.

"Let those who deserve it get what's coming to 'em," I said, "and may the rest be peaceful and enjoy the life they have. I think the Lord would agree with me on that point."

"We'll open the office and see if we can find any wanted posters. It's pretty funny them making us the law, ain't it, after what we did to that stagecoach driver?" said, Kid, pulling his six-gun from the holster, pointing at a rabbit running through an open space, and saying "pow, pow" pretending he was shooting.

"We shoulda told 'em false names, though. I can't believe I done something like that, shooting that man in cold blood and never muttered a word for his soul. I'm going to Perdition, banished by the Lord to everlasting Hell."

"You just have a guilty conscience. After a while, it becomes a normal way of life. Don't think about it, we're almost there." Kid gave his horse a slap and he took off at a trot.

The windows and walls of the Sheriff's Office were punctured with bullet holes, the door was open, and the inside was trashed. Even the rifles were missing from the rack and the cell keys stolen. The desk drawers were out and dumped on the floor upside down, the contents strewn about.

"Don't them scoundrels ever sleep?" asked Kid. "It has to be the Castanat gang that done this. We got our work cut out for us today, Bobby, gettin' this place straightened out, the window replaced, new keys and the door repaired."

"Finding glass around here to put in a window frame will be a miracle," I said, looking through the shattered remains. I saw a man trot by the window and into the office with a clump, clump of his boots on the floor.

"Sheriff, sheriff! I heard a helluva commotion last night with shootin' and shoutin' and horses clamberin' around. I looked out my window and saw that dern Serge Castanat git off his horse and break this door down. He and two others stole the rifles and made a helluva noise in here," Mayor Ned Pritchett looked at all the papers and drawers on the floor. "It's a wonder he didn't set fire to the place."

"They sure made a mess, Miser Mayor," said Kid. "I wonder why nobody shot at them outlaws. Doesn't anybody in Idle Springs have a gun? Maybe if they took a couple of shots at them, they would've left before creatin' these shambles."

"It only took 'em a minute or two, and everybody was in bed," said Ned.

"Is there any extra glass in town?" I asked. "And a locksmith? We gotta get this place fixed up before we can go chasin' them that done it."

"Nearest glass is in Fillmore on the other side of the mountain. It'll take a few days to get it. I can get the door fixed in a day or two and you fellers can put the office back together. You'll want to know where the paperwork is. I think we can get new keys made in town by the blacksmith. He does things like that."

Kid turned a quizzical eye on the mayor and was going to say something, but a man and woman were standing at the door looking at the destruction and us talking.

Pritchett turned to them, "Good morning, Nordell and Sofronia. We were just talkin' about a broken window. Are you here to see me or the new sheriff?"

"We heard the noise last night and came to take a look and meet the new sheriff."

"Howdy, folks. I'm the new sheriff, Kid Ferry by name, and this gent here is my deputy, Bobby Chase-the-Lord. How can I help you?"

"Sofronia thinks she knows you, Mister Ferry. Is he the man, Sofie?" said Nordell Garner.

"He looks younger than I imagined him," staring at the Kid and glancing at me. "The man I knew was named Ferry, but he was older and wore a dark beard. Have you ever been in Kentucky, Sheriff?"

"No, don't believe so, Missus Garner. Never been there."

"See, I told you it wasn't him," said Garner. "Come on, let's get out of the way so they can get to work on the office."

They no sooner left than Doc Sycamore entered, saying, "Ole man Castanat wants to bury

Junior on his ranch, Sheriff. Can I release the body or are you still investigatin' the matter?"

"What do you think, Mayor? Is it all right with you?" said Kid.

"He can bury him wherever he wants to. Let him go, Doc."

"What about Tubbins? You can let him go, too. The family better bury him before he wakes up and takes his star back," said Kid, chuckling at his little joke.

"Blasphemy is a sin," I said, gazing at Kid.

"I've already notified his wife," said Doc.

First to leave was Ned Pritchett after telling the sheriff, "I'll see if I can find somebody to make that trip to Fillmore."

The Garners followed the mayor out the door, not saying anything.

Doc Sycamore was hanging around with one eye on the sheriff and the other on me, picking up papers from the floor.

"Tubbins didn't have any next of kin other than his wife, Betty May," said Doc.

"I'm sure she'll give him a decent burial," said Kid. A small knot of people had gathered on the boardwalk in front of the office.

"What do you think these people want, Doc?" I said, standing with a handful of papers.

"I don't know. I'll leave you to deal with 'em," he replied, and walked out the door.

I followed Sycamore to the door and stuck my head out. Daphne Merik stood in line behind a tall, slim, older man wearing a gray mustache. She was the only person I recognized. She was holding a grain sack in one hand and a cloth purse in the other, looking tired with puffiness below her eyes. She was watching me.

"Excuse me, sir, I would like to speak to Miss Merik before I get to meetin' these folks," said Kid standing in the doorway by me smiling at the tall man.

"Well, go right ahead sheriff. I ain't in such a hurry to talk to you that I can't wait a couple more minutes," said gray mustache, winking his right eye.

Kid gave him a long silent stare that made him cringe. Kid took Miss Merik's arm above the elbow, saying, "Come in Miss Merik. I know you so you're first in line with me."

Leading her through the door after I stepped inside, Kid tried to close it, but it left a big gap. I pulled it open, smiled at her, and said, "How's your father doin' this morning?"

"He seems to be much better. He's up and about and sent me here to see if the sheriff could send a deputy out to keep a guard on the place. He's afraid those Castanats will be coming to see him again." She paused and watched Kid replace one of the side drawers in the desk. "I brought you and Bobby some boiled beef and bread for breakfast. You left too soon to eat with us," and handed him a burlap bag.

"Mighty beholden to you, ain't we, Bobby?" said Kid. "As to your question about a deputy, Trace Schneider will be showing up here shortly and I think he'll be able to ride out that way and talk to your father."

"I'd be glad to do it, Kid," I said, staring at Daphne. "You and Trace have things to do and I have something to talk over with both the Meriks. What do you say, Sheriff? You don't need me to help clean this place up now that we put the desk drawers back in. It's about done."

Kid looked me in the eye. He saw the affection I had for her and took his time making a decision. I'll bet he's falling in love with her, too.

Moving his eyes to Daphne and smiling, Kid said, "Well, Bobby, I don't know what you have to talk to the Meriks about, but I guess you can ride back with her and talk to her father about the men who beat him up. Is that all right with you, Daphne, er, Miss Merik?"

"That'll be fine Sheriff. Thank you. Are you ready, Deputy?"

"As soon as I get me some beef and bread," I said, digging into the bag. "I'm sure hungry."

CHAPTER ELEVEN

The Merik's Cattle Stolen

Eating on a beef sandwich, I followed Daphne out of the office. I put the food in my coat pocket while climbing onto my horse, Lawman. In the saddle, I grabbed it and took a large bite riding at a walk alongside Miss Merik. We never spoke until well clear of town.

Turning my head this way and that, I said, "It's a beautiful morning, isn't it? The flowers are in bloom, the birds are chirping, the sky is blue and only some low-flying clouds. No rain today." I looked at my female companion being jostled in the saddle by the big roan she rode into town. She was astride the horse like a man today, not side-saddle fashion.

"Beautiful, if only I could enjoy it, but I'm worried about my father home alone. What if those men show up while we're gone, Bobby?" She kept her eyes straight ahead. "I have a feeling they won't be so easy on him next time. They want our land for some reason and I'm afraid they'll do anything to get it. Have you ever been in a situation like this, Bobby? There ain't nothing of value on the property, other than the land itself, that we know."

Not answering her question, I said, "Well, they won't get it while I'm here to protect you and your father, Miss Merik. It'll be over my dead body, and I don't plan to die soon," I told her, admiring her profile. I could see her small, straight nose, determined lips, and her white blouse tucked into her flowered skirt, a black shoe in the stirrup.

"Oh, Mister Chase-the-Lord, I hate to put you in between those men and my father, but I don't know what I'd do without you and the sheriff, especially you riding home with me, to who knows what we'll find," she sighed. Her eyes on me, she continued, "Thank you. We don't have much to offer, only some home-cooking, and we'll share that, of course."

"That will be plenty, but I do have a request for you and your father. I'll tell you what it is when we get there," I said, smiling like an idiot.

She smiled back.

"I hope my father's fine and them neighbors haven't returned to push us off our land."

"We'll do our own pushing if we see them, Miss Merik."

"Let's go directly to the house to make sure father is all right," she said, twisting her upper torso to the left to get a better look at me. I was half a horse length behind.

A short time later, we tied the horses to the hitch in front of the cabin. Daphne was the first to enter, yelling, "Father, father, are you here?"

I heard Mister Merik yell, "I'm bringing in some milk. I milked the cows and herded them out to the pasture. I see you came back with the Indian. Anybody else?"

I winced. Good thing he didn't call me Injun.

We walked to the kitchen.

"No, daddy, Trace wasn't there and the new sheriff had his hands full. Have they been back again?"

"I guess so. We're missing most of our herd, Daphne. Somebody stole 'em or run 'em off last night. It's funny we didn't hear anything," said Merik, looking at her and moving his eyes to me.

I saw Mister Merik's swollen eye wash over me, his face bruised from the beating he took. I wondered how well he could see through that sorry orb.

"I'll take a ride around the ranch and see if I can learn anything." I hitched up my trousers and adjusted my revolver. "We didn't hear a thing in the bunkhouse after we hit the sack." I started to close the front door when Daphne cautioned, "Be careful, Bobby."

My heart took an extra beat climbing on Lawman.

I rode around the barn and headed for the trees up the hill, hoping to sight a trail over which the animals were herded. The sun passed its zenith before I spotted anything that looked like cow tracks leading away from the ranch. I stopped my horse and looked around to make sure of my bearings.

Seeing tracks going over a rise and away from Merik's place, I followed them for a couple of miles up and down hills and around a small lake, where they took a sharp turn to the northeast. Rocky ground made it hard to follow, so I left the trail and rode to the top of a hill, where I had a view of the valley.

"There's the Merik's place down there, and the town over there. The Castanat ranch must be that way, where the tracks are leading. I've seen enough for now. I can't go charging into that nest of sidewinders by myself," I said out loud.

I turned Lawman in the direction of the Merik's cabin and headed back to tell them what I had seen.

"Them tracks were going toward the Castanat's ranch. I followed them until I made sure," in answer to old man Merik's question. "I wasn't going to bust in on their little party alone. I think I'm good as any man with a gun, but it would be certain death going against that gang of thieves in broad daylight."

We were standing in the front room until Merik turned and headed down the hallway. I followed him. He turned into his bedroom, sat on the bed, and began talking.

"Well what are me and my daughter supposed to do, just let thim steal our ranch from under us? They'll be back, and next time they'll be out fer blood, and I ain't goin' to let 'em git any of it," Merik blustered. "Let 'em come and I'll blast 'em out of their saddles before I give up this ranch. Are you goin' to help us, Mister Chase-the-Lord, or hightail it back to town and git us some help?"

I stared at the old farmer from the bedroom doorway with a sudden itch to draw my revolver and plug him, but instead, I thought of Miss Merik and how pretty she appeared. I moved my gaze to see her through the doorway to the kitchen cutting a piece of meat. I stepped into the room and stood facing Merik.

"I ain't no coward, if that's what you're trying to say Mister Merik. I'll be here to help protect your property from being taken over by anybody. You can rest easy on that. I ain't going back to town. My pardner and I'll go get your cattle come dark, or my name ain't Bobby Chase-the-Lord."

Merik watched me closely while I spoke. He blinked and sighed and said, "Uh-huh," with a sarcastic nod of the head.

"I thought you might help me on a project I'm undertaking, Mister Merik," I said, with new enthusiasm. "Do you and your daughter know of any vacant buildings in town that I could use for a while? You see, I'm a preacher at heart and would like to spread my religion and give folks a chance to come to my church and hear what I have to say. I know the Mormons are all around here, but they're only one aspect. The Bible says there is room for everyone, and I want to add mine, too."

"No, we don't know of any empty building. This is a new place and folks build what they need. Maybe if you get a hold of Honas Johnson at the lumber mill, he'll saw you off some boards, and you can build your own church building. But don't go tryin' to convert me and Daphne. We ain't religious and don't belong to any church."

"That ain't too helpful. I was hoping you and Miss Merik would be the first to join, but the Lord takes His time. I guess you don't have a Bible you could loan me for a couple of weeks?"

"Of course, we have a Bible. No self-respecting family would be without," said Merik. "Daphne! Daphne! Get the Bible from the front room and give it to Mister Chase-the-Lord, so he can start his church. He can't get started on anything without a Bible. We never look at it anymore since you growed up and Ma died."

I heard Daphne come from the kitchen and start down the hall. She had only taken a couple of steps when a loud knock on the front door sounded through the small cabin. I heard the footsteps continue down the hall to the front door and a man said, "Is that deputy here Miss Merik? The sheriff wants him to get into town quick. He didn't tell me why. 'Jist find that deputy and tell him to git here fast,' he said."

By now, I was sitting in a chair next to the bed listening. I jumped up before Daphne could answer and yelled, "I'm here, Trace. What's happening in town that the sheriff needs me so dern quick? We were just goin' to have a bite to eat."

Daphne turned to go back to the kitchen with Trace following. "I don't know what's going on, Bobby. Like I said the sheriff wants you there pronto. Ya better saddle up and git to rollin'. He tole me to stay with the Meriks until further notice."

"I'm on my way. Can you fix me a sandwich, Miss Merik, while I get my horse ready? I'm mighty hungry."

"I'll get you some roast beef and bread and put 'em in a sack while you saddle up. I'll hurry."

I went out the door, slipped the knot holding Lawman, and climbed onto the saddle.

Daphne was standing on the porch ready to hand the sack to me. Grabbing it from her hand, I said "Thanks. I'll be seeing you." I pushed my spurs into Lawman and he took off like a gunshot.

CHAPTER TWELVE

A Castanat is Captured

We galloped into Idle Springs, never noticing the birch or cottonwood trees or anything else until Lawman slid to a stop at the hitch rail of the Sheriff's office. I dismounted and entered, wondering why I was needed.

"Look who I got locked up, Bobby," said Kid. "I caught him at the general store after all the hubbub died down this morning. He said he came into town to buy supplies for the ranch. Take a look in that cell."

I stood in front of the cell and studied the being lying on the cot with his hat over his face, dressed in a brown shirt and dirty canvas trousers. On his feet, were well-worn, brown western boots.

"Hm-m-m. Just who is he that's so important, Kid? I can't see his face."

"Why, that's one of those Castanat brothers lying there. Said his name was Willie, and he put up a fight, or at least tried to, but I had him handcuffed before he could say tits on a cow. Marched him here and put him in there. I think I'll hold him for ransom for that Serge feller. We do you think? Or should we just take him outside and string him up?"

"You could hold him for stealing the Merik's cattle, and we could ask the judge to hang him. Their cattle were rustled last night, and I followed their trail right to the Castanat ranch, practically."

"This is an open and shut case then. We won't wait for the judge to come through town. We'll let him go and shoot him for getting away. We won't waste the county's money by stringing him up. I'll put out a reward notice and collect that. No problem."

I turned away from the cell and began walking to the chair by the wall.

"You won't git away with a trumped-up scheme like that, Sheriff," said Willie, sitting up on the edge of the cot. "My brothers will come after me before you git a chance to do anything. I wouldn't be surprised they'll show up any minute now."

"Let 'em come we'll be ready. It'd make it easy for us, huh, Bobby?" the sheriff said. "We'll just round 'em all up and throw one or two in jail with you, if they survive long enough."

"You sure act brave. Wait 'til they git here, and we'll see what happens." Willie laid back down and replaced the hat over his face.

I sat in the chair in front of the desk and looked at Kid. Lowering my voice so the cowboy in the cell couldn't hear, I said, "How are we supposed to stop the Castanat gang from getting the prisoner out?"

"Well cross that bridge when we come to it," Kid said barely loud enough for me to hear. "Somebody made off with the Merik's cattle, huh? We'll have to split up for the night. One of us, namely me, will be at the ranch with Trace. We'll be watchin' out for those thieves in case they come again. And you, Bobby, will have to stay here and protect our jail mate for tonight. I don't think they'll hit both places, but we've got to stay alert just in case."

Disappointed, I stared at Kid and said, "I don't like it. I'd rather be at the Merik ranch flirting with Daphne. She was going to lend me a Bible until we were interrupted by Trace showing up and telling me to get into town pronto."

"You'll have plenty of time to make your case with her after we hang the Castanats, Bob," said Kid, using the short "Bob" for the first time like he was upset.

"I know but I wanted to strike while the fire is hot and ask her to join me in my church teachings using their Bible."

"Why don't you take a walk to the stable and get some shuteye in the hay so you'll be rested up for the night? We can't afford to leave this rustler by himself."

I heard the jingle-jangle of chains from a wagon or carriage hurrying into town and reached the door first. Opening it, I watched the stagecoach roll to a stop in front of the general store, raising a swirl of thick dust.

Listening, I heard the driver say, "I have some mail for the town," while watching him climb off the stage. He was a short, chubby man, with a growth of whiskers that covered his blue shirt front and wearing a Mexican-type hat with a wide brim. He reached through the coach window and pulled out a U. S. Mail bag, exposing his black wool trousers wet with sweat and thin from wear. Seeing the Mayor, he said "Here you go, Ned. I'm on my way to Richfield as soon as I get rid of this stuff."

Ned Pritchett said, "Howdy Abe. Thanks for the mail. Ya got time to wet your whistle, don't ye?"

"You buyin', Ned? If so, I got time," and headed into the store.

Pritchett nodded his head, "Why not?" and with the mail bag in one hand followed Abe into the building.

Kid joined me and we followed Pritchett along with a few residents to see if there might be some mail in the bag for the sheriff.

Ned brought a bottle from beneath the counter and handed it to Abe. Abe hoisted it into the air and drank a long slug and handed it back. Ned took a sip, screwed the cap back on and put it back on the shelf.

"I guess I'll be leavin' if that's all I'm gittin'," said Abe, looking at Ned and licking is lips.

"That's your usual, Abe, and all the time I got to give out free whiskey."

"Why, you cheapskate. I'll drink more next time."

Abe left the store and we soon heard him yelling at the horses, "Git-a-goin', ya dumb, four-legged scoundrels."

Pritchett opened the mail bag and glanced through everything before calling names. The third one called was Tubbins, the former sheriff. Pritchett handed the envelope to the Kid saying, "You might as well see what this is, Sheriff. It ain't no good to Sheriff Tubbins."

We waited, but we didn't get more calls for us, so we headed back to the office before opening the envelope.

"What d'ya suppose that is, Kid? It looks official to me."

We entered the office and Kid, plopping into his chair, tore open the envelope.

"I'll be a horned pig, if it ain't a Wanted Notice for us. Look what it says: 'Wanted, Kid Ferry, a White man and Bobby Chase-the-Lord, an Indian, for murder and theft. These two desperadoes murdered a stage coach driver named Karl Willets, stole the stage and horses and left for parts unknown. Armed and dangerous. If seen, notify the nearest U. S. Marshal's Office. Description of these outlaws and' . . . Hell," said the Kid. "They give a detailed description of us. What're we gonna do, Bobby?"

"First thing, get rid of that dodger and let's think on it for a while. We got to come up with a good excuse and fast that it wasn't us that done it, before somebody happens to see that thing at a post office or some place."

"Yer on to somethin' there, Deputy." Kid pulled out a sulfur from his front pocket, struck it on the side of the desk, and set fire to the Wanted Notice. He stared at me a long time after disposing of the ashes, from my head to my feet and back to my face. "I sure wish we could change yer looks, Bobby, so you don't come off as an Indian. We'll get you some new clothes and a different cowboy hat, but how we goin' to lighten you up? Yer skin is too dark to be a White cowpuncher."

"Can't help that. Maybe if I dress like a Mexican, I can pass as one. I'll grow a moostache and let my hair get long." I paused for a few seconds. "Hell, I don't know that language. I'll have to think of something else."

"Me, neither, Can't speak a word," said Kid, "but I can dye my hair black and, oh, the heck with it. We're goin' to have to leave this two-bit excuse for a town and find somewhere else to settle down."

"I got it!" I said, eyes wide open. "We'll turn ourselves in to the Marshal when we deliver our prisoner and explain to him that we didn't kill anybody other than help out this little town."

"Hah! I got a better idea. Split up. That's what we'll do. They're looking for two of us, thinking they'll find us together, but on our own, they'll never catch us. What do you think of that?"

I stared at Kid like he was crazy, my muscles tense. Why would he want us to go our separate ways? Were a stronger force together. I relaxed my muscles in my arms and legs. Taking a deep breath, I said, "All right, let's get moving. Where you going to go? I'm staying right here and tell the folks my real name, Guiseppe Brandetti, of San Francisco, a poor orphaned Italian."

"That's good, very good. Yah, you could pass for one of those Latin types, I think. All you have to do is convince 'em," laughed Kid. "I'm takin' your prisoner out of that cell and me and him are goin' to ride the outlaw trail. If you come lookin' for us, be prepared to fight, Guiseppe," and he winked his right eye and smiled.

CHAPTER THIRTEEN

Bobby and Kid Ferry Split Up

"If anyone asks, tell 'em I'm goin' to Richfield to turn Willie into the Marshal. But, I'm taking him to his ranch," said Kid. "I'll untie him and tell him I want to join up with his brother's gang of outlaws as soon as we get out of this shamble of a town. From here on out, yer on yer own, Bobby. Just remember some of the things I taught you."

I barely smiled, a little tic in my lips, and said, "Take the Merik's cattle back to their ranch and turn them loose. They don't need to be hurt in this."

"I'll do that, but I don't know what that gang has in mind for that ranch. I'll try to steer 'em away, before they do somethin' bad."

Standing in the doorway, I watched the Kid and Willie Castanat ride out of town, Castanat with his hands tied behind his back.

I re-entered the sheriff's office. "He helps me, I'll help him," taking a seat in the chair behind the desk. "Now, to get a hold of Ned Pritchett, our so-called Mayor, and tell him the real story."

Knowing the mayor would be by to see how things were going, I leaned back and hoisted my booted feet to the wooden desk, pulled my hat low, and concentrated on what to tell the mayor about the name change. Kid introduced me to this ruse and the stories always sounded logical. I'm going to have to make mine just as logical sounding, so I don't get a bunch of questions that I ain't ready to answer.

Soon, I had visitors. Daphne Merik and Trace Schneider walked into the office.

Standing up in a quick burst of energy, I said, "Miss Merik, what are you doing in town? And Trace, what brings you here? I thought you'd be staying at the ranch."

Trace said, "Daphne insisted on bringin' you a Bible. You tell 'im, Daphne, why we're here."

Digging into a cloth handbag, Daphne pulled out the well-used Bible that she went to fetch before I took off. "We brought this so you could get started on whatever you were going to do, and I have to pick up some things at the store. Where's the Sheriff?"

Reaching for the Bible, my fingers touched hers. Trying not to show my confusion, I said, "He arrested one of those Castanat people and is taking him to the Marshal in Richfield to turn him over." I stared at her pretty face for a second and just a tint of red came into her cheeks. "Thanks for the Good Book, Miss Merik, but I don't think I'll be needing it. You can take it back with you."

"I guess we came to town for nothing, Trace. Let's go to the store and go home. Trace is still my bodyguard ain't he, Bobby?"

"Why, yes, of course. Trace can stay with you until I get there later. I have a confession to make, Miss Merik and Trace. My name isn't Bobby Chase-the-Lord, it's really Guiseppe Brandetti at your service. Didn't know how long I'd stay here, so I pulled that name, Bobby, out of thin air. I've decided I like Idle Springs and am going to stay around for now. Things will be settling down after we catch the Castanat gang or they leave and go somewhere else to do there killing and rustling."

Trace and Daphne stared at me like I'm a little crazy.

Daphne said, "I was getting used to Bobby. Now you changed it to Guiseppe. I don't know whether I believe you or not."

Trace said, "Just who are you, anyway? Are you an outlaw and have to keep changing yer name?"

"Of course not. That's the truth. I was just using another name I saw in a paper until things quieted down. You can continue calling me Bobby, I'm used to it. My mother and father died of cholera, I been told. I ended up in an orphanage as a baby and stayed until I reached sixteen years old. So, there you have it. I'm glad to get it off my chest. I'll see you both later at the ranch. I'm expecting Mayor Pritchett any minute now, so you'll have to excuse me."

I sat in my chair and began shuffling papers on the desk with my head down.

Trace opened the door and waited for Daphne to leave first, but she stood in the same spot staring at me. She turned toward the door as Ned Pritchett entered.

"Good afternoon, Trace and Mss Merik," said the Mayor.

"Our new Deputy Brandetti is looking for you, Mayor," said Daphne and she and Trace left.

The Mayor didn't say a thing, but came into the office looking like he had something on his mind.

"Deputy, let's talk. What's going on? I saw the Sheriff leaving town with Willie Castanat. Where's he going? I thought he is supposed to keep those outlaws locked up."

"Well, Mayor, good day to you, too. The sheriff is taking that outlaw to Richfield to turn him over to the Marshal. That's all that's going on, except I've got something else to tell you."

"Oh, Richfield, eh? The Marshal, huh?" coughed Pritchett. "Good idea! What is it you want to tell me?"

"I haven't been truthful, Mayor, and I want to set the record straight before it gets too far along. My name is Guiseppe Brandetti, not Bobby Chase-the-Lord." Looking the Mayor in the eye, I told him the same thing I told Trace and Miss Merik. "And that's all there is to it. I didn't want to get started off on the wrong foot, since you engaged me as a deputy sheriff to dole out law and order, for which I am very grateful, Mayor."

"And very young to be a lawman, maybe too young. How old did you say you were, Bobby?"

"I guess I'm about twenty, or I will be come October, if I could believe those people at the orphanage. According to Father Connelly, I was sixteen when I left there, so I'll be twenty, Mayor. That's old enough to be a deputy, ain't it? You can keep calling me Bobby. I like that name better."

"I suppose age doesn't make any difference, and you proved it with your revolver when you came to town. There ain't no one faster around here. I was worried that our sheriff was going to hang Willie without a trial, but since he's taking him to Richfield, you'll have to be the law until he returns. Anything else happening in Idle Springs, Bobby? The town's not so Idle lately."

"Just me and them law books on the shelf. I better get back to them before the people think I don't know wat I'm doing? Thanks, Mayor Pritchett."

Pritchett left and I breathed a sigh of relief. Opening a law book, I began leafing through the pages but soon stopped and thought about what just happened. I slumped in my chair and I felt the blood leaving my face. I had strong feelings of remorse over what I just told the Mayor and before that, Daphne Merik and Trace Schneider.

I stared at the wooden floor and wondered what Sweeney would think of me and how am I ever going to face him again. How could I start my own church after telling all these lies, going back to the day I left home? Kid sure changed me, teaching me all the ways to break the law and get away with it, at least until I'm caught and forced to tell the truth. I'm a killer, a thief, and a gol-darn horse thief, too. I'm homesick, that's all it is. I stood up, pulled my hat down on my head, and left the office to take a tour around town, get a bite to eat, and shake these feelings.

CHAPTER FOURTEEN

Kid Ferry Joins the Castanat Gang

In the bright afternoon sunlight, I raised my eyes to the sky, noting the fluffy, white clouds that were building up in the west and would be casting shadows over the town in another half-hour. Maybe, rain, maybe a thunder burst coming. This being my first chance to really take a look at Idle Springs, I walked down the middle of the dirt road to the edge of town where the sagebrush, cottonwoods, beech trees, and scrub brush began to thicken. An occasional pine tree tried to reach the sky in the midst of all the other growth. I stared, admiring the greenery and the hills in the distance with the bluish mountains rising behind.

Turning away, I took a different trail behind the buildings where three or four houses stood. Two of the houses were bright white with new paint and two were older and needed painting. Cutting through an alleyway between the stable and blacksmith shop, I stopped to say howdy to the blacksmith, a large and muscular man. He reminded me of some of the miners back in Dry Creek, only his clothes appeared to be a shade cleaner.

The smithy stopped his hammer in midair and let it fall to the ground by his big work shoe.

"Well, if it ain't our new deputy," said the big pile of flesh, not smiling, more of a smirk on his dirty, black-streaked, sweaty face. "You followin' the sheriff with that outlaw? Yer kinda late and slow to catch him on foot." He laughed loudly, throwing back his head at his own puny joke.

"I ain't following them," I said. "I saw you slamming your hammer at that horseshoe and had to stop and admire the performance. My name is Deputy Brandetti, but you can call me Bobby. I wanted to thank you for the jail keys."

"Nice ta meetcha. You're welcome. I like to make little things like that, but chances don't come along very often. Now, if ya don't mind, I have work to do. He picked up his hammer and let it slam against the cooling iron on the anvil.

I watched the blacksmith hit the horseshoe two more times before I left and walked to the stable where I had my horse. Lawman gave me a quick glance of recognition. I gave him a swipe along his flank and a pinch of hay. Leaving him alone, I walked to the store. Looking in the front window, I saw the mayor with his back to me reaching for something on a shelf behind the counter. I quickly turned away and returned to the office.

"I'll go steer crazy if I'm destined to sit around here all day with nothing to do," I said to the four walls.

****

Well on our way out of town, Kid reached over, knife in hand, and cut the rope binding my hands, saying, "You're a free man, Castanat, but don't try anything stupid like pulling this gun I'm handing you. Let's go on to your ranch. I'll explain things to you and your brothers, and maybe we can make a deal. I'm no longer the Sheriff of Idle Springs. No, I plan to join up with you and make a little money on the outlaw trail."

We left Idle Springs behind an hour ago on the road to Richfield. Now, we turned our mounts toward my family's ranch and cut through the countryside at a lope, me leading. I was happy to have my revolver in its holster again and decided that going home was better than trying to shoot Kid Ferry. My brothers'll take care of him soon enough.

We rode into the ranch yard not long after and tied up at the hitch rail. Dismounting, I led the way into the house where we found my Pa and Serge sitting at a table in the big room. Serge jumped up when the door opened.

"Look what I brought home. They threw me in jail when I went into Idle Springs, and the sheriff was taking me to Richfield to the Marshal, but changed his mind and cut me loose, and here we are."

Serge stood with his hand on the butt of his revolver watching us. My father turned his head so he could see who came in, not saying anything.

"He wants to join our gang, Serge, he said. Pa, this is Kid Ferry, former sheriff of Idle Springs and one of those who shot Junior, but he swears it was the other one did the shootin'. I wasn't there, so I don't know. We can certainly use him, can't we, Pa? He is fast with that six-gun."

"We'll see Willie. At least you're free," said my old man still in his chair at the table. "Do you think we can trust him, Serge?"

"How come he's so anxious to join up with us? I don't know whether we should trust him or not, him being the law around here a couple hours ago," staring at Kid with an undaunted look on his face, the black pupils of his eyes small. "What is it he thinks he can do for us?"

Clearing his throat, Kid said, "You need me because I can keep the law away from here being the former sheriff, and with a gang like this, we can make some money. I ran the owlhoot trail before them stupid farmers made me a lawman. My friend the Deputy, won't do anything to us as long as I'm here. He ain't too bright when it comes to enforcing the law. To show you I'm on your side, we'll go into Idle Springs tonight and I'll leave that deputy something to think about. We can take over that town and run it like it was our own."

We Castanats kept our eyes on Kid while pondering what he said.

"I don't think that's a good idea either," Pa said, rubbing a hand through his gay hair. "Our hideout in the mountains is a better place to be running things from. Mister, why don't you make yourself at home in the bunkhouse for a couple of hours, while we make a decision whether to give you a shot in the gang or a shot in the chest. Willie will show you where to put your horse and where your bed is. Right, Willie? And bring the Barnett brothers back with ya when yer finished."

"You bet, Pa. Come on Kid, let's go see what we got."

CHAPER FIFTEEN

Kid Returns the Merik's Cattle

I locked up the office, got my horse, and rode to the Merik ranch, enjoying the peace and quiet of the countryside in the early evening. At the ranch, I related the day's events to Daphne and her father and Trace Schneider, emphasizing the new facts about myself. I knew my story was a little lame and repeated the part about being an orphan, hoping to gain sympathy.

"I'm still interested in starting my own church, but I feel that I have to put that aside for now and concentrate on helping the settlers of Idle Springs by continuing my job as Deputy Sheriff."

Schneider seemed disinterested and left for home.

We ate supper, not talking much, and I went to the bunkhouse.

Late in the night, I woke up startled by sound nearby. Sitting up, I reached for my .44 hanging in its holster from a nail in the bunk post. I almost had it when a match flared and a voice said, "Put yer hands back on top of the covers! We have to parley, Bobby."

I recognized the voice before I saw Kid in the dim light and dropped my hand from the gun butt.

"What're you doing here, Kid? I thought you joined up with the Castanats."

"Sh-sh, not so loud. I brought the Merik's cattle back, me and Willie, and I jist wanted to tell ya from now on, we're on different sides of the law. Here's my Sheriff's badge. The next time we meet we may have to kill each other. Jist wanted to give you notice that it's not personal, but never let yer guard down. I'm leaving now and may the best man win."

"But, Kid . . .," I began, but it was dark again. I heard the bunkhouse door close against the frame and knew I was alone.

I laid my head down on the pillow, agitated by this sudden development. I'll not only have Kid to look out for, but Serge Castanat and his whole band of outlaws. What are they going to do next? Take over the town? How am I going to fight 'em off with just my gun?

I lay awake for a time before falling into a light sleep. I dreamed the worst nightmare I ever had. The Castanat gang took turns shooting at me, and the Kid said, "Yer in fer it now, and I'll be shootin' last. Ha, ha, ha!"

I woke up in a sweat and immediately crawled out of my bunk and went outside. I washed my face, neck, and head in the cold water from a tub by the door. Grabbing an old, dirty towel, I wiped the water off, turned, and re-entered the bunkhouse.

Whew, that dream was too real I thought the Kid was going to let me have it.

Dressed and recovered, I walked to the Merik's house and knocked on the door. I looked around the yard and stared at the field beyond the corral in the fast-changing light of dawn. The cattle were munching on the grass, standing silent and content.

Daphne opened the door and said, "Come on in and look out. You can see farther." Her eyes were bright and shining. "I see somebody brought the cattle home last night. Who did that?"

"It wasn't me," I said. "The Kid talked the Castanats into it. He woke me up late last night and told me he had joined the gang and was going to ride the outlaw trail. He said he would kill me, the next time we meet."

Sighing, I followed Daphne to the kitchen where the elder Merik sat. Merik raised his head and stared at me, saying, "Sit down and have some breakfast. I heard what you said, Bobby - er – Guiseppe. What got the sheriff so riled up that he turned outlaw?"

"Your guess is as good as mine. The last thing I knew, he headed to Richfield to turn Willie Castanat over to the Marshal. He always has been a bit too rambunctious and never satisfied. I guess he was tired of living straight."

"Well what are you goin' to do now?" said Daphne. Her eyes watched me. "I'm sorry to see him go. I kinda liked his handsome face around here."

"I'm still the Deputy of Idle Springs and I plan to keep at it, Miss Merik. The town needs somebody to stand up for the law-abiding folks, and that's what I'm planning to do until I'm fired, no doubt about it."

We ate pancakes and bacon without talking. I knew Daphne had her eye on Kid and may be falling in love, but she wouldn't admit it, not even to her father. Now, she should drop that line of thinking and look for someone else to marry. Maybe an Italian named Bobby, but she wasn't going to fall for me even though I'm just as handsome as Kid. She may want someone a little older. Someone who is rich and will take care of her father when he gets too old to look after himself.

I watched Mister Merik fork in the last bit of pancake and say to his daughter, "That Kid Ferry is a better man than this young Italian – er - Indian in my opinion. I hope that you ain't thinking of him as a future husband."

"I'm not thinking of anyone right now, Pa. We got our hands full with this ranch."

"Hear that, Bobby? Women! She's just like her mother at that age. She could only think of getting married and having kids."

"I told you, I'm not going to marry anyone for a while."

I heard a loud knock at the front door and Daphne jumped up to answer it, saying, "Who could that be this early in the morning?"

I listened closely to hear who was calling on the Meriks at this time of day.

"It's Serge Castanat, and he's got his gun ready. Pa, he's headed that way."

I heard a noise at the kitchen doorway. Serge took a shot at me. The lead hit the wall at the other side of the room with a dull thud. I fell to the floor, pulling my revolver in the same motion and firing at the outlaw. One bullet glanced off the door frame, tearing splinters and the other hit the wall, missing everyone but coming close to Daphne, who had followed Serge.

Serge turned and ran.

By the time I got up and followed Serge outside, he had one foot in the stirrup. He turned his horse, and all I could see was his hat above the saddle and a hand on the saddle horn. They headed for the corner of the barn, Serge hanging on like an Indian.

I fired at the running horse, aiming just above the haunches at the head of Serge peeking over the saddle. The .44 bullet hit the horn above his fingers and zinged through the air. I ran to the barn, peered around the corner and saw the outlaw race over the top of a rise and out of sight. I fired a lone shot after the fleeing man as a warning more than trying to kill him.

CHAPTER SIXTEEN

The First Saloon is Built in Idle Springs

The small town of Idle Springs stayed quiet for the next month-and-a-half with the Castanats lying low. I used the time to get acquainted with the residents, visiting each store, shop, or facility at least once a week and reminding the proprietors they didn't have to worry about outlaws while I'm the law. I told them I will do everything in my power to keep bad people away while assisting the good people with minor chores and lending a hand. I'm a man of God and I follow a plan of righteousness to set a good example.

There came to town a free enterpriser who began throwing up a saloon along the main road on the opposite end of town from the jail. His name was W. Coogan Hanratty. I introduced myself and informed him I would not be patronizing the establishment.

"I don't drink the hard liquors, I hate Valley Tan and don't care for the most common of gut wasters, beer," I said.

"Well, don't let that keep ya from stoppin' in. I'm going to have an eatin' establishment, too, where you c'n git the best corned beef in the Territory. Yes, sir, it'll be a fine place to fill up w'en yer hungry, Deputy. Just call me Coog or Coogan."

"I'll be dropping in, all right, to make sure there ain't no trouble. Places that sell the Devils liquid draw nothing but bad people."

With that, I left him and strolled back to the office talking to the townspeople on the way, especially any pretty woman I managed to see. I even crossed the street twice to make conversation with the females I saw climbing from wagons or crossing the road in the horse and wagon traffic. For a small town, it was getting more people and busier every week that went by.

I no sooner made myself comfortable in the sheriff's chair than in walked Mayor Pritchett.

"Bobby, I jist heard some startling news from the stagecoach driver. He tole me that he heard the Castanat gang robbed a train on its way to Salt Lake last Saturday. They got away with three thousand dollars in gold and shot three train workers, killing one."

"I wonder why he didn't tell me," I said.

"I dunno, but that gang of thieves own a ranch not far from here. Are you going after 'em, Deputy? They'll be robbing our town before you know it, if you don't do something to stop 'em."

"I can't act on rumors, Mayor," looking into his eyes and standing up behind the desk. "I have to wait until I get official notice that a crime has been committed before I can arrest anybody. If any of that gang comes to Idle Springs and raises Hell, I'll be right on his back, and when I get the notice that they're wanted men, I'll go after them. Don't know of anything else I can do right now, Mayor. Do you?"

"If they show up in town I expect ya to haul 'em to jail and throw away the key." Pritchett turned to leave.

"He must be getting ready to put in a bank," I muttered after the Mayor got out of earshot. "Why else is he so riled up?"

Sitting in the chair, I lifted my high-heeled cowboy boots onto the desktop. Pulling my .44 from the leather hanging down over the side of the chair, I checked to make sure it was fully loaded. I've been living at the Merik ranch since I came to town, and it's getting a mite boring. Helping out with the chores hasn't done me a bit of good with Daphne, but they haven't asked for rent money, either.

She's been ignoring me and missing meals. She cooks something and goes to her room. Ole man Merik ain't no better. I think his mind is going haywire, sitting there and staring off into the distance and barely eating enough to keep a hummybird alive. He rides a horse around the ranch and helps milk in the evening, though.

I stood up, adjusted my holster, and left after locking the office. I ambled around the corner of the building and ended up in the small barn where I kept my horses. Throwing a saddle on Lawman, I cinched the straps to my liking, threw some hay into the manger for the other horse, climbed into the saddle and headed on the road to the Merik place.

After eating supper and still sitting at the table, I told Merik, "I'm moving into town where I'll be close in case of trouble. I'll pack my stuff on my horse in the morning early and head on out. You'll tell Daphne, won't you? Tell her thanks for letting me stay here and the things she did for me, cooking and even washing my clothes, and thanks to you for your hospitality. I'll see you around when you come to town for supplies and stuff."

Merik looked at me with a blank stare. "I'll tell her, and we're glad to see you go. Maybe I can get Daphne to brighten up and be her old self again with nobody around to distract her. See ya in town, Bobby – er – Guiseppe – er – whatever your name is."

I gazed at him and saw that blank look return to his watery, bluish-green eyes. I arose from the table and left.

Packing up, I ran across that blue dress we were going to get altered, but never did, and there isn't a dressmaker in town yet. I wonder if it'll fit Miss Merik. No, she won't take it and she'll ask me a bunch of questions like where I got it and stuff. I better put it back in the saddlebag.

The sun wasn't up when I rode out the gate. A touch of gray in the eastern sky showed above the mountains to the east. The day is dawning. I traveled for a short distance, stopped, and looked back at the small house. A light flared in a window. "I'll see you in town, Daphne," I said, turning Lawman in the direction of Idle Springs and galloping away.

Arriving in town as the sky brightened, I unsaddled Lawman and threw my poke on the pile of hay. In the office, I left the door open for the light and sat at the desk wondering where I was going to sleep tonight. Starting to lift my boots to the top of the desk, I heard shots from somewhere nearby.

I jumped up, ran out, and stood on the boardwalk listening. Heading down the boardwalk, walking fast, I heard a string of shots coming from the other end of the road and someone yelling, "Yahoo, atta boy! Let 'em have it!" I ran toward the noise, taking long strides, my arms swinging at my sides. I pulled my revolver and a second later I was standing at the corner of the stable and staring at W. Coogan Hanratty, Mayor Pritchett, and a couple of other men setting off firecrackers and throwing them into the middle of the road.

They watched them fire off and yelled and laughed and carried on like school kids. Holstering my .44, I said, "What's the meaning of this, Mayor? What's going on?"

"This is Coog's big celebration and saloon opening day, Deputy. He just opened his doors to customers, and we're settin' off a few fireworks. That's all."

Coog yelled, "First drink's on the house today, Deputy. Let's go inside and have a drink."

"Thanks, Coog, but I'm on duty. I just came running when I heard all the noise."

Moe citizens were gathering to watch the show and followed Coog into his new establishment.

I turned around and ambled in the direction of the office, but stopped in mid-step in front of the general store to stare at two riders entering town at a gallop. I placed both feet on the boardwalk and watched as the riders slid to a stop by the hitch rail in front of me.

Kid dismounted, yelling, "Howdy, Sheriff."

Before answering, I watched Willie Castanat climb down from his saddle and step toward the walkway, thinking this might be my last day alive. I'll have to be on my toes. They would shoot me in the back and not give me a chance.

"Well, hello, Kid, and Willie Castanat. I thought you were in jail in Richfield, Willie. Ain't that where you're supposed to be?"

"The Marshal didn't have enough evidence to charge me with anything. Kid joined up with us and been working on the ranch herding cattle, Deputy. Kid and me been good friends since he came to the ranch."

"I heard rumors that the Castanat gang robbed a train up north, but haven't received any official notice to that effect. That's why I ain't paid a visit," I said. "You and Kid ain't welcome here, so I recommend that you buy your supplies and leave town pronto before you cause any trouble."

Kid watched, a smile on his handsome face, saying, "We heard the town has a new meetin' place and we intend to help celebrate its grand opening, don't we, Willie? Don't worry, Joe, we won't cause you any trouble, at least not today," he laughed.

"You talking to me, Kid?" I said, staring into Kid's eyes. I adjusted my revolver in the holster and folded my arms across my chest.

"Why, that's you, Guiseppe. Joseph is the Americanized name, so I called you Joe. That's all right, ain't it?" said Kid, standing easy and smiling

"Ain't nobody called me that for a long time. I just wanted to make sure you were talking to me, Kid. Joe sounds better anyway, but no one else has figured it out yet. You can just call me Bobby. I still expect you boys to be peaceful while in town."

I turned and started for the office, turned back to see Willie grabbing for his pistol. Kid held his wrist before he could get the .45-70 free of the holster.

"Don't be a fool," said Kid, letting go of Willie's arm. "You shoot him in the back, the law will hang you for sure. C'm on, let's buy our stuff and go have a drink at Hanratty's saloon."

CHAPTER SEVENTEEN

Trace Schneider is Elected Sheriff

When I returned to the office, Trace Schneider, sitting in a chair by the wall, said, "I saw you parleyin' with Kid Ferry and Willie Castanat. What are they doin' here?"

"They came into town for supplies for the Castanat ranch. Kid said they weren't going to cause trouble. I told them they were not welcome and to head out as soon as they got loaded up."

"Well, I sure don't trust either one to do what you want, especially that Castanat boy. He and his brothers been raisin' Hell since they came to town," said Trace, as I sat down in the sheriff's chair.

"I trust Kid to do what he says. We been friendly for a while, but one of these days, I will be forced to put him in jail or shoot him. He as much as told me that. I heard rumors that he was involved in a train robbery up north and as soon as I get something official, like a Wanted poster, I'll bring him in."

"Abe Duggins, the stagecoach driver, will be bringin' mail again one of these days," said Trace.

"Maybe you'll get something when he shows up. He always gives that stuff to the Mayor first."

"I hope so. The Mayor oughta appoint you sheriff, Trace. You're better qualified than I am, and you know all these people, where I'm just getting acquainted. I'll ask him about it next time I see him."

"Hell, I got my own problems with my ranch, but my boys are gittin' old enough to handle most of it. The sheriff is supposed to be elected. You should ask the mayor about that, and let the residents choose who they want."

"Good idea. I'll do just that. By the way, you don't need to spend any more time at the Merik place. Kid told me he returned the cattle and said they wouldn't bother them anymore."

The stagecoach rolled into town the next afternoon and Abe Duggins handed me, not the Mayor, a couple of envelopes addressed to the Sheriff of Idle Springs. Returning to the office, I locked the door behind me before I opened the mail. A handwritten complaint, unsigned, about the saloon, I found in the first one. Whoever wrote it, wanted Coog's tavern closed. "It ain't a good moral influence on our young people," he or she wrote. I'll give it to the mayor and let him worry about it.

I stuffed it back into the envelope and set it aside on the desk. I picked up the other one Abe gave me. It was from the U.S. Marshal's office in Salt Lake City and held four Wanted dodgers, one of which was for the arrest of Serge Castanat and his brothers and Kid Ferry for train robbery and murder of one Dale Harper, train guard.

I re-read the sheet and sat back in the chair, closing my eyes for a few seconds. I reached into my front pocket and extracted a sulphur and struck it on my trouser leg before putting it to the paper. The fire started in the lower left corner of the poster and flared into a small blaze consuming the entire sheet. I dropped it to the floor before my fingers got singed and stomped on it. Nothing left but charred, black ashes which scattered with the stomping. I stood up from the desk, grabbed an old broom from where it stood in the corner, and swept the ashes into a dust pan. I carried it to the door and threw the ashes into the street, most not getting there, but floating away on a breeze.

I noticed that things were settling down in Idle Springs and the cold weather began to turn the tree leaves yellow and orange and colors in between. Mayor Pritchett put out a notice announcing the election, telling everyone election day would be the first of November. The notice read: "The election is for the offices of Mayor, two council seats, and the Sheriff's job."

Pritchett wasn't pleased that I wasn't running for sheriff, telling me I had his vote as the best man for the job.

"Trace Schneider is the better man, Mayor," I said, looking him in the eye. "I may be the fastest with a gun, but Trace appears to have all the other traits that a good lawman should have, while I'm just a wandering soul looking for a place to establish a church. The Mormons have pretty well got Utah sewed up and I may be moving on at any time."

I don't believe Pritchett believed me, but dropped the subject and didn't bring it up again. He had his own battle to fight to hold onto the office of Mayor. Mister Hanratty threw his name into the pot.

He wanted the Mayor's office so he could open the town to more drinking and more liberal ways.

The election came and went. Pritchett retained his seat by three votes and Schneider was the new Sheriff. The two council seats were taken by Herod Watkins and Nordell Garner, founding citizens.

It snowed once before Thanksgiving Day, maybe a half-foot and it melted over three days, leaving the roads soggy and boggy, making walking and wagon travel difficult. The skies were gray the next few weeks with the sun peeking through the clouds enough to melt the snow and change the dirt to mud. Farmers with little to do slogged into town and spent time in the stores and more in the saloon drinking their beer and Valley Tan in quantities beyond reason. Trace and I were busy quelling arguments, stopping fights, and investigating an occasional shooting.

I took it all in stride, remembering the mining town I came from, which was much worse. I still lived at the stable, having cleared out a section in a corner and threw up a wood partition for privacy. I paid the stable owner six dollars a month, ate meals in the saloon café, and tried to make time with Daphne Merik on her trips to town without her father.

Kid and the Castanats seldom visited, going to Salina for their supplies, the Kid told me the last time I saw him.

Kid asked, "How come you haven't been out to the Castanat ranch and arrested the gang? You know they're wanted for train robbery and recently the bank robbery in Ephraim, don't you?"

"We haven't got any official word about it," I lied, "As soon as we get notice, we'll be after you."

"Maybe you've grown too timid with nothing to do but throw a drunk out now and then," said Kid, smiling. "Ya know I'm mixed up with Serge and his brothers and we got more plans in mind. How're you and Daphne gittin' along? She tole me that you been very attentive to her needs when her Pa ain't around. Don't git too close to her, 'cause I'm going to marry her pretty soon. Do we understand each other?"

"What I do is my business, Kid, and I don't want any interference from you or anyone else. Got that?"

Kid turned around mad with the worst look he had ever given me and left the stable not saying a word.

He ain't going to intimidate me by talking about marrying Daphne. I'll be after him as soon as I get a warrant, and we'll see who is going to win. I walked through town to the sheriff's office and told Trace, "If those Castanat brothers cause any trouble, I say we arrest them and throw 'em in jail."

"It has to be pretty bad trouble, 'cause I'm not goin' to git shot over some loud noise or them shooting up the bar, or somethin' that doesn't hurt anybody," replied Trace, looking up from the papers on his desk.

"We'll have to face them sooner or later and I'm not getting any younger," I said.

"Jist don't go off the handle without a good reason."

I glanced at the empty jail cell and turned my head to look out the window at the muddy road and the few people walking around. Nothing held my eye for very long. I propped my chair against the wall and sat down, closed my eyes like I was going to take a nap. Instead, I said, "I want an excuse to shoot Kid Ferry."

The sheriff looked at me, but didn't say anything.

"He told me he was going to marry Miss Merik, but I ain't going to let him. She's too nice a girl for him."

Trace eyed the papers on the desk and picked one up, ignoring me.

"Here's something you can do, if you're gittin' too restless. It's that Wanted flyer for that Barnett kid that's been layin' around here for a while. Gary Barnett, wanted for goat stealing, twenty-dollar reward for return of four goats belonging to Vern Landis of Sigurd. Three black and white and one white."

Trace grinned and held the notice out for me to read. "Might take a while to find those goats, but you can find Barnett out by the Castanats. Let's take a ride out there."

"I'll meet you at the stable. I'll tell the mayor on the way that we'll be out for a couple hours or more," I said, dropping my chair to the floor and standing up. I took the dodger and walked out the door.

CHAPTER EIGHTEEN

Goat Herding

Arriving at the Barnett ranch, we slowed our horses to a walk, pacing over the rocky ground and stopping near the front porch of the clapboard house. Sheriff Schneider dismounted and tied his horse to the hitch rail. He saw Aaron "Iron" Barnett standing on the porch with a defiant look on his tanned face.

"What's on your mind, Sheriff?"

"We need to talk to Gary, Mister Barnett. We got a Wanted notice that said he stole some goats. Is he around?"

Iron Barnett looked at me.

"So, this is the famous gunman I heard shot Junior Castanat and a couple others, is it? How come he didn't run for Sheriff, Trace? He'd make a better lawman than you."

"He doesn't know who lives in Idle Springs, and it's none of your business. Where's Gary before I lose my patience?"

"He ain't here. Hasn't been here for a while. He got a job workin' for Serge Castanat," said Iron. "You'll find those goats out in the field around that hill over there," pointing with his right arm, "He likes goats for some reason I don't know, and this is the third time he brought some home. He told me he bought 'em. Hell, you can go git 'em fer all I care. He's a real hothead, Sheriff. If you're goin' after him, be careful, he'll shoot you on sight. Since he got mixed up with the Castanats, he's uncontrollable and unpredictable. He shot Ike Howard over some trivial thing about them damn goats."

"Thanks for tellin' us, Iron. We'll find 'em and take 'em home, and we'll be looking to arrest Gary. You tell 'im that. Good day, Iron."

Trace mounted his horse. "Let's round up them animals and take 'em home."

We barely reached the field where the animals were, when Gary Barnett started yelling at us.

"Hey, if you touch those goats, you're a dead man," he yelled, galloping near. He stopped about fifty paces away and had his revolver aimed at the sheriff. "Jist back off and turn around. Nobody gits near my goats, ya hear?"

"Yer a strange man, Gary Barnett, putting yer life in danger fer a couple a damn grass-nubbin, skinny, lousy, milkin' goats. We're takin' 'em home to Sigurd and if you think you can stop two of us, you'd better think again," said Trace, showing a side of him that I hadn't seen or knew about. He looked angrier than a rattlesnake and just as menacing.

Barnett looked at both of us, sizing up his chances. He must have thought they were pretty good. He shot at Trace, but Trace jumped from his horse and raced for a dip in the earth. Barnett missed him three times before I shot him in the right arm. His weapon fell to the ground and he almost fell from the saddle. Managing to hang on, he spun his horse around and galloped away as fast as it could run like the scared coyote he was.

I started after him and Trace yelled, "Let 'im go, Bobby. Well get him later."

Stopping, I watched Barnett disappear over a hill, his shot arm resting on his hip. I returned to see if Trace had been shot.

Trace was climbing on his horse and when he got settled, he said, "All this over five damn goats! Come on, Bobby, let's git 'em on the road."

Neither one of us said a word until we had the animals headed toward Sigurd. Trace spoke first, "Gary Barnett is crazy like his father said and the sooner we round up the Castanat gang, the better it will be around here. Look, Bobby, we both don't need to herd these animals to Sigurd. I've got somethin' else I need to do. Jist keep 'em on this road and you'll run into the Landis farm on the south side of that town."

"Fine, if I don't shoot them all before I get there. How far is it?"

"Not that far, you should be back in Idle Springs about dark."

Sigurd was further than Trace told me, but I did make it back before midnight after eating an early supper with the Landis family and taking my time on the way home.

Idle Springs was quiet, except for the shouting and singing coming from the Hanratty Saloon. I stalled my horse, giving him a good rubdown and hay. I walked through town, checking doors and windows and ducked into Hanratty's to see what was going on. Making my way to the wooden bar in the rear, I leaned against it on my elbows and faced the half-empty room. Glancing at the front windows, nothing appeared but the blackness of the night. There were card games going adjacent to each other The racket came from those two tables.

"Who're those cowboys at that table, Coog?" I asked, turning my head to look at the bartender. "I ain't seen them before."

"Two of 'em are Iron Barnett's boys and the others said they are from the Uintahs and buying cattle from the Barnetts. They came into town to celebrate the deal, according to Ishmael Barnett. He's the one with his back to you."

"How much they had to drink?"

"Hell, I ain't been countin', maybe four or five beers and a few whiskey chasers. They been here since . . ."

Coog was interrupted by Ishmael Barnett standing at the table and yelling, "Gol dern you, Earnie, that's the second time you said you were cheated in that deal, and I don't intend to take it anymore. My Pa's an honest man and you ain't goin' to insult 'im like that. Grab yer iron!"

I was a second too late getting to the table. One of the Uintah men beat Ishmael to the draw and two bullets hit him in the chest He was dead before he hit the dusty floor. But Ishmael got off a shot on the way to the floor, hitting the Uintah cowboy above the right eye, killing him. The dead man fell on the table before slamming onto the board floor.

I waved my arm at the grayish-white smoke to clear it and pulled my revolver, yelling at the men standing around, "That's enough, fellers! Put your guns back in their holsters or you'll meet the man at the pearly gates."

"We ain't doin' nothing, Sheriff," said one of the Uintah men. "Earnie and Ishmael been argyin' all afternoon and there was nothin' we could do to stop it. I'm sorry, Caleb, that Ishmael was killed," he told the other Barnett. "We'll take Earnie back home and tell his family. Hell, we jist came to buy some cattle and these two start shootin' each other."

Caleb Barnett was standing with his Colt out, waving it in the air, "Ain't your fault, Jessie, but my Pa is goin' to be awful upset about it."

He put his .44 in the holster and sat down at the table leaning on his elbows. "You and Chip better clear out and git the cattle headed out. I'm goin' to have another drink while the doctor takes care of Ishmael. That'll give you time to get away before I tell Pa."

"You heard him boys," I said. "There ain't nothing the law can do. They shot each other at the same time and both are dead as rocks. You better get out of town before Iron Barnett hears about it, you Uintah boys. He won't take this sitting down."

The two Uintah men left, and it became quiet in the saloon. A man at the other table said, "Good thing you were here, Depity, only two dead. Bring us another round, Coog."

"Sorry, boys, I'm shuttin' down fer the night. I've had enough noise and killin' fer a while," said the bartender, wiping off the bar and shaking his head. "As soon as Doc comes and takes care of Mister Barnett, I'll be heading for me own kit."

I holstered my .44 and went back to leaning on the bar while waiting for Doc Sycamore to show up. Caleb Barnett sat at the table in the same position he took after the shooting. The men at the other table were quietly talking. They all stood up and left at the same time.

"That's the first killing we've had since you opened up, Coog, but I don't think it will be the last," I said.

CHAPTER NINETEEN

Bobby Flirts with Daphne Merik

The next morning, I showed up at the office as usual. Trace was talking with Daphne Merik about the weather it appeared, hearing Daphne say, "It was colder this morning than it . . .Well, good morning, Deputy Brandetti, is it now?"

"Good morning, Miss Merik. No, it's just Bobby. I haven't used Brandetti in a while. Nice to see you again. How's your father getting along?"

"He's fine. I stopped in to see how you were doing? Is everything going good with you? I wanted to ask you about Kid Ferry. Is he okay?"

I looked at Trace and dipped my head in a greeting and turned back to Daphne.

"Well, I haven't seen him since he got mixed up with the Castanats. We heard that gang robbed a bank in Ephraim, and I expect Kid took part in that. We'll have to arrest him, if he ever comes into Idle Springs again and we have a warrant."

Daphne looked disappointed, but said, "I guess you have to do what you have to do, if he was involved. What made him join up with that gang of outlaws?"

"Your guess is as good as mine. He's got a wild streak in him. It's real nice to see you, but I have to discuss something with the Sheriff, if you'll excuse us. I don't mean to be rude, Miss Merik, but it's important."

"I have to be going anyway. Pa wants me to get some headache powders from the doctor and pick up some supplies for the ranch. I'll be seeing you again. So long, Trace and Mister – er – Bobby."

After the door closed behind her, I eyed Trace in his chair behind the desk and Trace stared back. "Did you hear about last night, Trace?"

"If you mean the shootings, yes. I heard about it at breakfast at the café. Doc Sycamore told me what happened. I'm glad we don't have to get involved other than you writing a report about it. I'll betcha ole man Barnett will be charging in here before long demanding something be done to catch his son's killer. He knows damn well it was self-defense and the killer's dead, but he feels he's gotta do somethin' or have us do somethin'. There ain't nothin' I'm goin' to do about it, and you?"

"All I'm going to do is write a short report and file it. I figure we didn't have any laws broken, so it's over as far as I'm concerned. But what're you planning to do about Kid and the Castanat gang? Are we going to go hunting for 'em?"

"We can't go chasing around the country for outlaws in this weather, Bobby, unless they come into town and start somethin'." Trace lifted his boot heels onto the desktop and leaned back. He took off his hat.

"Well, I hope they stay away, myself. I'm going to take a walk around town and grab a bite to eat. I ain't had breakfast yet."

I left the office after Trace said, "See you later, then."

Hoping to catch up with Daphne Merik and ask her to have breakfast with me, I found her leaving Doc Sycamore's house.

"Miss Merik, would you like to get a cup of coffee or something to eat? I'd like to talk with you a minute, if that's all right."

"We going to that new café? I haven't been in there?"

"Yes, ma'am, that's the only decent place to go. Now, tell me what's wrong with your Pa that you had to see Doc Sycamore?"

She smiled and said, "Winter's been awful hard on him the last couple of years, so he asked me to pick up some liniment or something for his rheumatism and something for a headache. His arms and legs get awful stiff and sore."

"That's a relief. He's still fairly young for a man his age, you ask me."

We walked along the boardwalk without speaking, lost in thought. I was looking at her and thinking she was a real pretty gal with her blue eyes and quick smile and a dimple in both cheeks. Her reddish lips seemed ready to break out in a smile, whether I said anything or just gazed at her. We walked past the café without realizing it. It is a small place, only four tables and a counter with four stools. The kitchen was behind the counter, and you could watch the cook get your meal ready on a grill.

"Woops! We went right by the coffee place, Miss Merik," I laughed.

"I was too busy thinking to notice, Bobby. Let's have a cup of coffee and a piece of pie."

We sat at a table by the window, passing a man and a woman at another table on the way.

Coog had hired Missus Danich to run the café, a short, nice-looking, clean-clothed woman with short blond hair. She was the only employee, waiting the tables and cooking the meals, too. Sometimes service came slow, but this morning, she was caught up, having only those two other customers.

"Good morning, Miss Merik and Deputy. What can I fix you today, coffee, breakfast, tea, or a piece of cake or pie freshly baked?"

"Have you any apple or cherry pie, Missus Danich?" said Daphne.

"I have an apple pie just out of the oven. Is that all right?"

"You bet."

"I'll have my usual, and lots of coffee for both of us," I said.

Missus Danich headed for the kitchen twitching her short hair.

I turned to Daphne and asked, "When was the last time you saw Kid?"

"Maybe three or four weeks ago. Why?"

"I ain't seen him since that one night in town. He's got himself fixed up with the Castanats and is heading for trouble."

"I shouldn't tell you this, but I feel that I have to, Bobby. I was falling for him when he came by the house. We took a long walk and talked. I thought he was going to ask for my hand, but he didn't. He said if I wait for him until he gets enough money together, he will be back. I told him I would, but I'm beginning to have doubts about it. I don't want to marry an outlaw."

"Well, if you're asking for my advice, I'd tell you to wait, but I'm doing it for my own selfish reasons, Daphne. You should wait and see how things are going to turn out."

She stared at me like she had never seen me before.

"He may not be coming around for a long time I can't wait forever, but for now I'll take your advice." She gazed into my eyes and waited for a response.

"I think you're a smart girl, Daphne." I smiled.

Missus Danich brought our food and we ate it with very little talk. I walked with her to the store and held the door open while she entered.

"Thanks, Daphne, and be careful if Kid comes around." Reluctant to let her go, I watched her stop at a rack containing women's clothes before leaving.

I returned to the office in a happy mood, smiling all the way and looking the people in the eye as we passed, but not really seeing them.

CHAPTER TWENTY

Marshal Phinley Visits Idle Springs

Trace and I were sitting in the office later in the same day, when the door opened and a stranger entered. At least I never saw him before. Trace jumped up, saying, "Well, I'll be derned, Bib Phinley, how you doin'?"

Bib, unbuttoning his coat, smiled at Trace and gazed in my direction.

Turning back to the sheriff, "Fine, Trace, just fine. Things been calm in Idle Springs? I heard you were the new sheriff, and I see you have a new deputy. I heard that Sheriff Tubbins was killed by somebody named Castanat. That true?"

"Yes, he was. I was sorry to see it, but they made that Kid Ferry the sheriff, since he saved the town from further injury and then Kid quit and joined up with the Castanat gang. My deputy, Bobby Chase-the-Lord, was the head lawman after that, until the people voted me in. Now, we got two officers of the law and I got a hunch we'll be needing more. What brings you up here, Marshal Phinley?"

Bip Phinley shook my hand while Trace talked. He stared at Trace now and said "Well, I'm looking for any of that gang that robbed the train and the Ephraim bank. I have warrants for 'em and I'll need help roundin' 'em up. Can I count on you to provide some men and supplies?"

"You bet you can," said Trace. "I'll put out the word for a posse to meet here at sunrise tomorrow morning, and we'll see who shows up, this being a small town. Is that soon enough? I'll take you to the Castanat ranch and their hideout and see what we can find, Marshal."

"I have warrants for Serge, Willie and Wiley Castanat, and Gary Barnett, Caleb Barnett, Jug Wilson, and Ishmael Barnett, and somebody that calls himself Kid Ferry or somethin'. There's a two-hundred-dollar reward for Serge Castanat and one-hundred each for the others. Me and my men will be here before sunrise prepared for a week of ridin'. Meantimes, I'll be at the café or at our camp on the edge of town by the stable."

"Fine," said Trace.

"We'll let you know how many men we git. Bobby, you wanna take a look in the saloon for anybody that wants to go for a ride?"

"I'll walk with the Marshal to the café and see what's goin' on in Coog's place," I said, looking at the sheriff and the marshal. "If you're ready, Marshal, we'll get started on the posse."

With a nod of his head, the marshal left and I followed.

Phinley stopped in the dirt of a small alleyway and said, "I didn't mention it in there, Deputy, but I have another warrant fer somebody called Bobby Chase-the-Lord. Supposed to be an Indian out of the northwest. You heard anything about him?"

"Not really, but I been using that name since I came to Idle Springs. Picked it up in Great Salt Lake as a joke, thinking it would sound better than Guiseppe Brandetti and I look like I could pass for an Indian. But I never saw him, met him, or anything like that. Just picked it out of a newspaper, is all. What did he do that caused a warrant to be issued?"

The Marshal started walking again, stepping up onto a section of the boardwalk. I hurried to keep pace.

"He's wanted for robbing a post office. I don't suppose you know anything about that?"

"Uh-uh, don't know nothing about a post office being robbed, was it around here?"

"Nah, it was up north near Salt Lake."

"I came down from Salt Lake, me and that Kid Ferry, but we ran into a Daphne Merik being attacked by this Serge Castanat and his brother, Junior. Junior was killed in the process of us freeing her, and we delivered Serge to the sheriff here. But Serge took off and got away and we've been looking for him ever since, Marshal."

"Oh, I heard about that, all right, you know how news travels I heard that your ridin' partner joined up with the Castanats, too. What made him do a thing like that? Is he the real Kid Ferry?"

"I can't tell you for sure, Marshal. He told me he didn't know what his real name was and we were both orphaned as babies, so I just don't know. I only knowed him for a short time."

"We catch 'im and we'll find out whose tellin' the truth. The first thing I want done is to round up those train robbers and bank thieves, and we'll figger out who this Kid Ferry is."

"Here's the café Marshal. I'm going next door and see if I can recruit a posse in there. I'll see you later."

I held the café door open while Marshal Bib Phinley entered. I watched him choose a table next to the front window before closing the door.

I have to be careful around him and prove my name is not Bobby Chase-the-Lord somehow. Maybe if I can show him I'm not a robber or outlaw, he'll believe me.

I went into the saloon through the swinging doors and walked right to the bar.

"Howdy, Coog. Pour me a stiff one before I make an announcement to the people in here."

Never having drank straight whiskey or any other kind of alcohol, I picked up the jigger and downed it in one gulp. I coughed and could feel my face turn red. Holding my hands to my chest, I squeezed my eyes shut. A couple of tear drops began running down my cheeks. I put my hands on the bar edge and pushed against it, breathing deep.

"Damn, Coog! Why didn't ya tell me that stuff was strong? I ain't ever drinking anymore of that poison. Give me a glass of water and hurry up about it."

Coogan was laughing his head off, but poured me a glass of water from the pitcher on the bar. Still smiling, he said, "What's this announcement yer goin' to make, Deputy? Anything important?"

Paying no attention to the question, I drank the water in three gulps. Composing myself, I turned around to see who was in the place. There were three men playing cards at a table by the front window. I didn't know them by name, but I'd seen them around town. Taking a deep breath, I said, "Gentlemen, Sheriff Schneider needs some help to round up the Castanat gang. Marshal Phinley of Richfield is here with some men, but he said he needs more. We'll be leaving at sunrise in the morning to go look for 'em and he'd appreciate it if you joined the posse. Bring enough supplies to last a week and plenty of ammunition. Marshal Phinley has warrants for the gang. If we don't get rid of this gang of thieves, Idle Springs will be in for a hard time. As a Deputy in this town, I would appreciate it, also, if you lent a hand in this venture. Like I said, we're leaving at sunrise. Be at the Sheriff's Office a little before. Thank you."

Coog said, "I didn't know you were such a speechmaker, Deputy. I ain't goin' to be closin' up for anybody to go chasing around after a bunch of outlaws, but I wish you luck."

I returned to the office and told Trace and took a seat in the chair by the wall.

"That ain't going to be much help, but we'll see who shows up," said Trace.

CHAPTER TWENTY-ONE

The Posse Hits the Trail

I stood behind a large cottonwood and watched Bib Phinley deploy the men, seven total with the two volunteers from Idle Springs, Curly Daniels and Wilfred Barney. The posse covered three sides of the Castanat ranch house, leaving the backside open, since it was next to a large hill. If anybody escaped out the back door, he could be seen running up the hill or coming around the side.

Bib and one of his men he called Tex said they would knock on the front door, while the others found something to stand behind, a tree, a barrel, the corral fence, etc.

Trace stayed in town in case the gang showed up. I thought I should've been the one in town, because Trace knew where the Castanat's ranch is located. But Curly Daniels said he knew ole man Castanat well and had visited him a few times.

Bib and Tex dismounted and tied their mounts to the hitch rail in front of the long porch. I looked at the house and corral and at Bib Phinley almost at the porch steps. There was no fence around the house or the outbuildings. The only fence was the one we came through about a mile back that appeared to mark the property line. No curtains hung over the two front windows of the house, and not much paint left on the outside. It looked streaked and weather beaten. No flower garden, just dirt and rocks passed for the front "lawn."

Bib and Tex were at the front door, taking up stations on each side. Bib rapped on the door and waited for someone to answer. Not hearing any noise from inside the house, Bib started to turn away when the door opened silently, exposing an elderly gent with a long, gray beard and hair, dressed in a black suit and white shirt with a black string tie.

The old man and Bib exchanged a few words that I couldn't make out. Bib and Tex left the porch, remounted their horses and headed away from the house. Bib yelled, "They ain't here," and waved his arm around, signaling to the men to get mounted and follow him. They stopped at the gate and waited for the men to gather around. I drew up and halted a few feet away, facing the Marshal, Curly Daniels, and Wilfred Barney. The other posse members were not far behind.

"The old man said that Serge and the boys left a couple days back and didn't tell him where they was goin'," Bib said, loud enough for everyone to hear. "I don't have a warrant for the old man, so I can't arrest him. According to him, Serge is the leader and he don't tell him what's going on anyway, so he don't get in trouble. He said they could be in Moab or eastern Utah, or Montana as far as he knew. Does anybody know where their hideout is?"

"I think they have a place not too far from here, in the mountains over there," said Curly

Daniels, pointing to the east where the humps of some mountains ran north and south. "I can lead you there and see if the gang is hiding out. I heard they had a small ranch up one of the canyons where they run cattle."

"It's worth a look-see. Lead the way and we'll be right behind you," said Bib.

Later in the day, the posse pulled to a halt in the very spot that Trace, Kid and I had stopped earlier to look over the country.

"Take a look down there at that stream, Marshal, and follow it with your eyes to that canyon over there," Daniels said. "I believe that's where the hideout is."

"Just look down there. Nothing is moving, not a breath of wind, no birds even. We better keep our eyes open for an ambush. Follow me down one at a time with some space between us," said Bib. Guiding his horse over the rim, he started down the slope, keeping in the trees as much as possible.

I went over the rim last, ensuring that the entire posse followed the marshal. I didn't know the men very well and didn't want anyone slipping off in the trees and heading back to town. I had a feeling we were going to need every man-jack to capture the gang.

"I'd rather be over-cautious than lose a life," the Marshal said to the posse grouped around him safely at the bottom. "Keep your eyes open and spread out as we move along this creek into the canyon."

There was no need for the extra caution.

"I reckon we are the only humans around," said Bib, staring into the depths of the canyon.

A cold breeze picked up, blowing in our faces and refreshing spirits and bodies. Bib raised his left arm, signaling us to gather around him once more. I pulled Lawman to a stop and watched. The breeze was chilly and I tucked my coat around my neck.

Bib said, "There don't appear to be anything in this short valley. Turn around and let's retrace the trail to the creek and go further up that other canyon. If we don't run across some sign that the gang is around, we'll go back to town and plan our next move."

It was a waste of time going into the other canyon. No sign of outlaws in the area or any other life that would indicate a ranch existed near here. We reversed directions and headed for Idle Springs.

The sun, obscured by gray clouds, dropped near the western horizon by the time we got close to town. We stopped at the Merik ranch, watered horses, and let them feed on the grass.

Bib told the Meriks what we were doing as he sat on the porch steps talking to them, "We didn't find hide nor hair of any outlaws or any cabin neither. You wouldn't know where that gang hides out, would you?"

"No, Marshal," said Daphne. "We only know what Idle Springs knows. The rumors are that they have a hideout somewhere in the mountains, supposedly not far away."

"You heard anything different, Mister Merik? You traveled up there more than once, hain't you?"

Merik replied, "I haven't been in them mountains for two years or so, Marshal. They coulda built a city up there for all I know. We told the deputy that the Castanats want our ranch for some reason, but they haven't been back yet. They're not welcome here."

I stood by the Marshal, listening. The others milled around or leaned against the porch and talked among themselves.

I said, "There's a horse coming and he's coming fast. Listen! He's in a big hurry, Marshal. He'll be here in no time. Look, he's turning in." I raced toward it, yelling, "Hold up! Whoa!! Whoa!"

Members of the posse rushed to corral the horse. The Marshal grabbed the bridle and walked in a circle, calming the animal.

Trace Schneider was hanging on to the saddle horn, leaning over the side like a desperate man. He let go of the horn and fell to the ground with a loud moan, "They got me and I lost a lot of blood. It was . . . Serge Castanat . . . and his boys, and . . . Kid Ferry . . . shot me. They took over Coog's saloon and are raisin' Hell. . . with the townspeople. They shot the Mayor, too."

The Marshal knelt and picked up Trace with both arms. "Look! He's been hit below his right collar bone. No wonder he's lost blood. Let's git him into the house and fix up this bullet hole and ply him with laudanum. Miss Merik, you and yer Pa take care of him. We're goin' into town as soon as we git him settled."

I had the cold shudders going into the house. Is this to be my death, taking on the Kid tonight? Has it finally come to this? I guess we should git it over with. I watched Bib drop Schneider's body onto the bed. I checked my revolver, not looking at anyone, trying to overcome the lingering fear. Which one of us will die tonight?

In a calm voice, although my insides were twisting, I said, "There he is in bed, Marshal. Let's go catch that skunk that shot him," not letting the men know I lacked confidence. I didn't want to kill my best friend or be killed by him.

CHAPER TWENTY-TWO

Shoot-out in the Saloon

As the posse approached the outskirts of Idle Springs, I watched Marshal Phinley raise an arm in the air and yell, "Whoa! Hold up, men! We can't go riding in there in a bunch. Half of you go around to the other end of town and tie your horses to a bush or somethin' and just walk into town like nothin' is wrong. We'll wait here for fifteen minutes to make sure you have enough time. We'll saunter down the sidewalk and keep the Hanratty Saloon covered.

"Deputy, you know that Kid feller, so you stay by my side and point 'im out. You keep that Serge feller in your sights. If we can git the drop on them two, I think we'll have 'em."

The town was quiet, no one roaming the streets. Our boot heels echoed in the night, tromping toward the saloon. Following the Marshal, I moved onto the dirt of the road to make less noise. I saw the other members of the posse sneaking along, keeping in the shadows and walking tiptoe against the buildings on the boards of the walkway. Drawing closer to the saloon, the Marshal waved to one of the men to cover the back entrance.

I looked through the front window and saw the Kid lifting a glass of beer to his lips. I smiled, seeing the black beard and hair of Kid, knowing it was that black shoe polish he bought in Great Salt Lake. I said, "Marshal, that's Kid Ferry drinking a glass of beer and the gent beside him is Serge Castanat."

I heard Kid laugh loudly at something Serge said. Coogan was behind the bar looking annoyed at the goings-on, jaws tight and his blue eyes moving from one outlaw to another. Leaning on the bar with both hands, he held a rag in his right hand.

Gary Barnett, his right arm in a sling, and Willie Castanat were sitting at a table with partly filled beer glasses in their hands. Barnett took a swig and set the glass on the table.

The Marshal drew his revolver and said, "Let's go."

Shoving the swinging doors aside, he walked to the bar in a confident stride, his spurs clinking and boots chunking on the sawdust covered floor. I was right behind him.

"Well, if ain't the famous outlaw, Serge Castanat, and part of his gang. You are all under arrest for several crimes, including robbing trains, banks, and killing innocent people."

"You got the drop on us, Marshal," said Serge, "but look out behind you!"

The Marshal wasn't falling for that old trick, saying, "Drop your guns and . . . "

A shot came from the hallway leading to the back door. Bip turned, firing his .44 and fell to the floor. Wiley Castanat stepped from the hallway firing at anything that moved and everyone was moving now, drawing artillery and plugging away with one thing in mind, shoot the sons-a-guns before they shoot us. Seconds later it was over.

I shot at Serge and fell to my knees. A bullet whizzed by my chin, hitting my ear lobe and scraping out a groove in my neck and jaw. I keeled over and sat down with my revolver smoking. Kid laid on his back, his eyes wide open, a hole above his right eye and one in his left chest. He was laying on top of Serge, a trickle of blood leaking onto Serge's black wool trousers below the left knee.

I saw Wiley Castanat laying on his front, not moving, three holes in his back, blood oozing out, soaking his wool coat.

I turned my head toward the bar just as Coogan raised up with a shotgun in his hands, aiming into the crowd. I followed his gaze to the piles of humanity that were no longer able to drink his Valley Tan. The bodies were laying at odd angles, their revolvers in hand smoking and leaking the ash-gray luminescence into the air, bleeding life's blood into the sawdust from holes in the chest, head, arms, and legs and bellies. One had two holes in his back, heart high.

What a bloody mess! Turning my head away, I saw the Marshal bleeding from his back, blood dripping into the sawdust from his torso.

Looking at the front door, Wilfred Barney, from his position by the batwings, closed an eye and stared at the bodies. In a sudden frenzy, he shot Gary Barnett. His revolver smoking, he returned it to his holster and walked to Bib's body, checking to see if he was dead or alive. Hearing moans, we stared into the lessening smoke at Willie Castanat on the floor, reaching for his revolver that had fallen out of his hand.

"Don't do it, Willie, or I'll plug ya," said Barney, his hand on the butt of his tool of death.

Willie pulled his arm back, coughing blood, and tried to see who was talking. He passed out before saying a word.

I heard one of the Marshal's men, "We need a sawbones for him, but the rest are dead, except for the deputy. He needs some help, too."

I sat on the floor, gun in hand, looking at Kid now, my eyes wide open with watery sputum seeping from my mouth, blood dripping off the left side of my neck. I unconsciously put my left hand to my ear.

Foggy from gun smoke, it was hard to see in the dim light from the one fluttering lamp hanging from the ceiling, swinging back and forth. Deathly quiet for a few seconds, I moaned and looked at my bloody hand, raised my pistol, aiming into the smoke at the dead body of Serge Castanat. I moved my .44, aiming at Kid, but seeing he had met his maker, I dropped it to rest on my leg.

Well, Kid, your outlaw life is over. I'm glad the Marshal shot you and I didn't have to. I had my hands full with that damn tricky Serge, and he almost got me. Sorry it ended this way, but we were caught up in something we couldn't control. If I live through this, I'm quitting the law and going to California and start my church. I'll be a preacher and a man who follows the teachings of Jesus. Maybe Daphne Merik will come with me.

THE END

About the Author

Born in Altonah, Utah, in 1932, he began writing Westerns around the year 2000 after composing books on family history and genealogy. He is a member of the Arizona Authors Association and the Western Writers of America. He retired to Sun City, Arizona, with his wife in 2001 and enjoys the desert life.

Take a look at his blogs:

www.oscar-curlyblog.blogspot.com

www.oscarcasebooks.com (Cattle Dust)

Sign up for his Newsletter at either blog or on his Facebook Author Page.